I find myself constantly referring to
something I call the Beginning.
"For want of a better word, I guess
I'll have to stay there, for a few
emotional beats, before I go on to the
upper levels of purgatory.
"The strong, always tired, black dirt
working robots, who happened to be
my parents, and all of the relatives
who looked and acted pretty much as
they did, were not the Beginning, nor
was the clapboard shack with the old
newspapers wadded into the cracks,
nor was the white man who had the
power of life and death over us.
"No, it was the aroma of places
I'd never smelled, the look in a pair
of eyes I'd never seen, the urge to
wander around inside my soul.
That was the Beginning."

CHESTER L. SIMMONS
(THE GREAT LAWD BUDDHA)

ODIE HAWKINS

Originally published by Holloway House Publishing Company

Copyright © 1990, 2012 by Odie Hawkins

Front cover photo by Zola Salena-Hawkins,
www.flickr.com/photos/32886903@N02

ISBN: 978-1-5040-3585-9

Distributed in 2016 by Open Road Distribution
180 Maiden Lane
New York, NY 10038
www.openroadmedia.com

*To Phavia Kujichagulia,
fellow writer, fellow spirit,
with love.*

CHESTER L. SIMMONS

Chapter 1

Sherman, Willie Burkes, Herb, Bobo, Billy Woods and Chicago Daddy, junior members of the Afro-Lords, lounged around on the front steps of Miss Rabbit's apartment building, puffing on cigarettes, surreptitiously passing a fifth of cheap wine around as they dealt with the passing scene and tried to forget that tomorrow was Monday, meaning school.

Phillip Mayflower, the neighborhood "sweet," strolled past, his head held high, the muscles in his slender face twitching as he tried to ignore the homophobic attitude of the Afro-Lords.

"Watchu up to, Mr. Lady?" one of them called out to him.

Mayflower stopped and made a dancer's turn, hands on hips.

"I'm mindin' my own business, 'kay? And leavin' yours alone, 'kay?"

The gang members, enjoying any kind of scene, tried to

agitate the drama.

"Yeah, I heard that!"

"Tell 'im 'bout it, Mr. Sweetthang!"

Mayflower gave the whole group a well cultivated look of disdain and pranced on down the street, past Chester L. Simmons, a.k.a. The Great Lawd Buddha, and his woman Josie, having one of their too frequent disagreements.

Josie, her words slurring past a pint of vodka, talked loudly into Chester's left ear.

"Now lissen here Buddha! If I've told you once, I've told you a hundred times! I'm not gonna keep on goin' through all these changes with you!"

Mayflower nodded pleasantly at the couple, a smile of pure amusement dimpling his cheeks.

"Hi, Buddha! Hi, Josie!"

Buddha turned from Josie's spiel in his ear with a grim look on his face.

"Hey May, what's to it?"

Josie flashed a brief smile, "Hello Mayflower," and turned back to her number with Chester L. Simmons.

"Awright, now you just tell me! Just tell me what makes you think you too good to work?! Just tell me, 'cause I sho' as hell wants to know!"

Chester L. Simmons, the Great Lawd Buddha, a deep-clefted series of frowns wrinkling his brow, topped by a grim expression covering the rest of his face, spoke to Josie from between clenched teeth.

"Josie! Goddammit! I *am* workin'! I'm doin' my thang! Why should I waste my time on some jiveass job when it prevents me from doin' my very own thang, huh? Answer that, if you can?"

"Bullshit! You just lazy, that's all. You don't wanna work!"

Chester, Benin-Mao masked face, touched delicately at his

10

polka dotted orlon ascor, pulled his ivory-bone cigarette holder out of his breast pocket, gently screwed a French cigarette into the end of it, and stood back from Josie, better known behind her back as Miss Heatwave.

"Josie, look, all this jaw jackin' is counter-productive. You go on upstairs. We'll talk about this some more, when you calm down a lil' bit."

Josie, knuckles on her hips, pouted her bottom lip aggressively, looked Chester up and down as though he had leprosy. Or stank!

"Why can't we talk about it now?"

Chester leaned into her pout and blew a stream of smoke into her face, slowly. "Cause now ain't the right time. We'll talk later. Now why don't you go on upstairs and cool off? I'll be up in a little while!"

Josie skewered her eyes up hatefully, stuffed the urge to say something super nasty and turned, with every eye on every lush curve, to clack click up the apartment house stairs.

Chester, shaking his head from side to side in a caricature of disgust, looked from one young face to the other.

"Women! Can't do with 'em, can't do without 'em! What was it the philosopher Nietzche once said? 'When you got to women, carry the whip'."

He looked from one puzzled face to the next, an amused gleam in his eyes.

"What're you youngbloods doin' out here this late? Plannin' some kinda offbeat crime or something?"

Bobo, giggling foolishly at the attention being paid them by one of their favorite people, answered for the group.

"Nawww, Buddha, nothin' like that. We just chillin' out, drinkin' a little Bird, that's all. You want a taste?"

Chester nodded no, wrinkled his mouth up at the sight of the bottle.

"Not for me, sports. That would tear a hole in my guts.

11

What kind of wine is that anyway?"

Chico Daddy supplied the title for one of the current ghetto-pop favorites.

Chester unwrinkled his mouth into a sarcastic smile and announced to the group, "That isn't wine, my friends. Chateau d'yquem is a wine, Beaujolai's Villages '86 is a wine, that shit ya'll drinkin' is just a bunch of chemicals them people stirred round in a vat and shot some carbonation into. Why don't you dudes put your coins together and get some good wine?"

The Afro-Lords looked blankly at each other.

"Shiii-it! We had to struggle to get this!"

"Go 'real!"

Chester's smile widened affectionately.

"You lil' po' ass motherfuckers! Here!"

He pulled a five dollar bill from his pocket and held it out to the group.

"Who's gonna be the runner?"

All eyes rested on Shedman, who reached out proudly for the bill and skipped away like a gazelle.

Chester watched him turn the corner to the neighborhood liquor store. "He'll git one o' those winos to cop for him for a quarter."

He slowly settled on the steps, sighing as his bottom touched the stone, made an elaborate ritual out of tapping the butt of one French cigarette out of his ivory-boned holder to replace it with another.

One of the members of his attentive audience leaned over with a light. He took a few long leisurely drags.

"Terrible fuckin' habit," he announced. "I got to give it up one of these days."

Four heads nodded in agreement.

"Any of you youngbloods ever been to China?" he asked suddenly.

12

Chicago-Daddy cocked his head to one side, like a curious dog. "China?"

Billy Woods moved down a couple steps. "Where? China?"

Willie Burkes, his eyes glazed from the last pull on the previous bottle, slapped in, "Nawww, ain't nobody here ever been nowhere, not really. You been to China, Buddha?"

Chester suavely pushed twin streams of smoke through his nostrils and nodded casually, yes.

"Uhhh huhhh. Where I got my nickname. They took one look at me and decided that I looked like The Enlightened One, The Buddha. Naturally y'all stuck that Great Lawd part onto it. Who went to cop the vino?"

"Sherman."

"Here he come."

Sherman, barely breathing hard, sprinted back up the street, clutching a brown paper bag with two bottles of cheap wine in it.

Willie Burkes and BoBo snatched a bottle each, uncapped it and started passing it around Chester.

"Where's my change?" he asked, taking note of another cheap brand going around. "I thought you were gonna get some good wine?"

Sherman handed over the change reluctantly.

"Uhh, well, there's five of us and one bottle of good wine don't go too far."

"What's good wine?" BoBo asked, bringing the bottle up to the side of his mouth.

"Hah! One good sign is that it costs at least four dollars 'n somethin' a bottle or it has a good name. For example, Cordon Rue du Splap or Fun Wha do Coo Coo or Shedon Chateau Splode."

The bottles circulated as Chester pedantically whipped off a series of French-sounding names.

BoBo, high again, winked conspiratorially at Chico Daddy.

"What was you starting to say about China, Buddha?"

"China? What about China? I missed that runnin' to get the pluck," Sherman said.

"Buddha was startin' to tell us that that's where he got his nickname, that right, Buddha?"

"That's right."

"What, I mean, why'd you go to China?"

"Mississippi was the main reason," Chester answered deadpan, as the Afro-Lords cracked up around him. "Actually, it was just a little bit more complicated than that. But to keep it simple, even though Mississippi is the very best reason I can think of. Let's just say I got on a boat one day and wound up in China."

The second floor window above their heads opened and Josie leaned out, her mouth curbed into a vicious line.

"Chester! You gon' stay down there all goddamned night?!"

Chester roared back, "I'll be down here 'til I git ready to come upstairs!"

Josie cocked a long, mean hard look at him and abruptly slammed the window shut.

Chester turned back to the group, shaking his head sadly. "Lawwd, ain't women hard to deal with?"

"Really!"

"Yeah, that's the honest to Gods truth!"

"Uhh, when did you leave outta China, Buddha?"

"Oh, ahhemm, that's a little bit less complicated than the way I got in. Actually, in a way, I was forced out. What happened is that I was livin' in this palace 'n shit, with this young princess. Her ol' man had been slain in a war with one of the Mongol tribes, and the next thing I knew, them crazy-ass Chinamen had started to revolutionize 'n what not. To make a long story short, I beat the princess outta ten

14

pounds of pure jade and split to Europe.''

"Europe?! Why Europe?!''

He took a long reflective look at his interrogator.

"Well, I'll tell you something. I'd jumped on a ship, going anywhere, and wound up in China, and when the shit hit the fan in China, I figured, what the hell! I been overseas for a while, why not stay over? I was hip to the East, you dig? Why not check out the West? One thing was damned certain, I sho' as hell wasn't goin' back to Mississippi.''

Sherman splattered a swig of wine on the people around him, laughing "Hahhhahh, hahh hah.''

"Hey! Watch watchu doin' man, you spillin' all the wine.

"Soooo, Europe it was,'' Chester cooly continue ignoring everything but his past.

"What was it like?''

"Well, I tell you, you youngbloods have to keep in mind hat the Europe I knew then may not be the Europe of today, or the Europe some of you all will discover when you get here.''

"What was it like for you, Buddha?''

"Clean outta sight! Somethin' else! Like I said, I'd managed to get my black ass outta China with this jade 'n all, thinkin' I was home free. But the first thing I know, I'd been rooked out of my jade by some slick talkin' Armenian cats runnin' the most sophisticated Murphy I'd ever encountered, and instead of landing in Europe richer than Carnation cream, I wound up in Marseilles on pure ass, hat in hand, stumblin' round lookin' for a way to git down.''

"Where's Marsay?'' Chico Daddy asked, shyly.

"It's a...uhh...it's a port city in France, lil' brother, a port city. And I'm gon' tell you right now, if you ever want to go there, don't try it on a Greek freighter like I did.

"We must've sailed half way round the world, stopping here and there, unloadin' shit here and droppin' shit there,

15

before we finally made it to France. If I hadn't been a young man, like you all are now, I probably would've died from eatin' all that wormy bread 'n shit. I think that's why my stomach is all messed up now. Anyway, by the time we got to Marseilles, I'd already decided to cut the freighter loose. If I'd stayed on the bitch too much longer I'd a either have starved to death, caught a red hot case of the bubonic plague, or been nibbled to death by the rats. Hard to say which.

"Believe me, it was a truly wretched experience, wretched."

He paused to replace his cigarette. The Afro-Lords paused in their bottle circuit.

"I jumped ship five hours after we docked, and started lookin' for a way to get down. Awright, I'm in the city of Marseilles, fantastic booyea base, and after two or three days of hustlin', scufflin', doin' a lil' this 'n that, I managed to catch a fantabulous Tahitian chick named Daisy and a place to hang my hat.

"The next thing I looked around for was a way to make some grand theft dough. Well, I didn't have to look too far. Some Algerian dudes—they're somethin' like the Mafia over there, them and the Corsicans—got in touch with me to act as a go-between.

"My job was to get together with sailors comin' in from the Orient and make deals for the dope they were smugglin' in for the Algerians. It had all kinds of dangers and pitfalls, but I stuck with it for about two months, 'til one day I got greedy and..."

"What kinda bread was you into, Buddha?"

Chester L. Simmons tapped ash from the end of his cigarette before answering.

"Ooohh...somethin' like eight, nine hundred bucks a week, big coins for the time. But that's where the problem was, you see? I just couldn't see myself makin' peanuts

16

runnin' the risk of getting busted and spendin' fifty years in the Bass-tille, while those motherfuckers at the top were steady rakin' in anywheres from 75 to a hundred grand a week.

"So, first chance I got, I palmed a half pound of uncut heroin, fresh from the laboratory, by way of Turkey, and split, along with my women.

"By this time I had collected a regular harem; I had Daisy, the Tahitian fireeater, a big ol' fine Alsation broad named Yvette and a lil' jet black diamond of a sister from Senegal named Mademoiselle Diop. She was so black that her gums was black, and talk about fine!

"Didn't nobody have to tell me Black was beautiful when I copped her. I could see it with my own eyes!"

Billy Woods, his eyes brightened by wine, asked in an awestruck voice, "Buddha, how much dope did you say you cut out with?"

"Half a pound, give or take a few grams."

"Oh wow! A whole half pound of smack."

"That's right, Lil' bruh, one half pound of pure heroin."

The second floor window socked open again and Josie leaned far out over the ledge.

"Cheessster! Goddamnit to hell! Are you gonna bring yo' jive ass up here or not?! I'm not gonna be yellin' out this window all night long!"

"Woman! I told you! I'll be up there when I get up there!"

Josie mumbled a stream of profane things down on him and slammed the window, rattling the pane.

"See there! That goes to substantiate a theory I've had for years: Don't get yourself involved with one woman, lil' brothers. Get three or four, but never one; there really is safety in numbers."

"Yeahhh, Buddha, I can dig where you comin' from!"

"Uhh, about that dope. How much was it worth, you

know, a whole half pound?''

Chester, his lip corners pulled down in haughty fashion, answered, "Bout a couple million, uncut, you dig?

"Mannnnn, a couple million!"

"Gawwwdammnnn!"

"Anyway, I split with my ladies. Had to cut Yvette and Mademoiselle Diop loose, excess baggage, no pun intended...hah hah...and believe me that was one of the hardest things I've ever had to do. I held onto Daisy 'cause she had some relatives in Paris that I could deal my shit off to.

"Paree! Paree! S'il voo play! Magnifique! Enchante! Hey, gimme some of that rot gut pluck!''

Two bottles, three quarters empty, were thrust out to him, gallantly. Chester snatched the nearest one, took a long wino's swallow.

"Uggghhh! I don't see how y'all can drink this shit, terrible as it tastes.''

He took another long professional gulp and continued, breathlessly.

"Now dig it! Here I am, in Paris, a queen of a city! In one hand I got half a suitcase full of monies and in the other hand I got half a pound of uncut hoss, and one of the planet's hippest ladies trailin' me like a love struck puppy dog. I'm really in a bag, you dig?

"I know I got to do several things quickly. One of the first things I got to do is get rid of all these narcotics because ain't no way I can get it 'cross nobody's border, 'cause them Algerian gangsters don't be jivin' and I know they gonna be on my ass like white on rice, soon as they discover that I have absconded with all their drugs.''

He paused for a quick swig on the bottle, absentmindedly stuck another cigarette into his ivory holder.

"Within a week, Daisy had put me with her cousin's brother, or her uncle's nephew, or somebody, and I had managed to deal off my stuff for two hundred and fifty million old francs.''

"How much would that be in real money?'' Willie Burkes and Billy Woods chorused together.

Chester casually adjusted the polka dot ascot around his neck.

"Ohhh, 'bout half a million dollars, give or take a few hundred grand.''

The Afro-Lords, leaned back on their elbows, eyes glazed and shiny from the pluck, astounded by the figures.

"I started to hold out for a million, but I thought, what the hell's the difference, really, between a half million and a whole million, 'specially since I was flirtin' with Instant Death (no replay) every day I stayed in La Bell Fronce. So, I settled for half a million and got on.''

"What did you do with the Tahitian broad?''

"I...uhh, I stuck ten grand to her, gave her one last hard supersonic fuckin'—and sent her on down the road. Had to. It would've been too easy for us to get racked up together. Can you see it? A little potbellied, slant-eyed Black man and this big ol' fine Polynesian princess. Can y'all dig where I'm comin' from?''

"Uhhh huh!''

"Yeahhh, I can dig it!''

"Sure hated to part with that chick too. She was really a righteous lady. I think she went back to Tahiti and opened up a saloon.''

He paused for a swig, looked off into his memory, daydreaming.

"Humph. Where was I?''

"You were gettin' off the set.''

"Yeahhh, that's right. I decided to make the Scandinavian scene.''

"The who scene?''

19

"Denmark, champ, Copenhagen, to be exact. It was the spring of the year and everything was happenin'. I could see why people called it the Italy of the North. I can remember walkin' through Tivoli gardens, a big old amusement park they got over there, tippin' my lid to every fox in the place and damned near gettin' ripped off every time I flashed my smile on somebody.

"It was a real groove. But I still felt kinda shaky, 'cause I knew the Algerians wouldn't be givin' up if they had the slightest chance of doin' some payback. And they're the kinda dudes who pinch your nuts off and stuff 'em in your jibbs, and then they torture you to death."

Several pairs of knees subconsciously drew together.

"Sounds like a cold-blooded bunch o' dudes."

"You got that right, buddy. But I wasn't too much bothered. I had everything I wanted. I was livin' like a upper class Vienesse pimp in a swank hotel downtown, spendin' money like it was goin' outta style, and to top it off, within a month I had copped an I-talian contessa who had more bread than I did."

'Mannnn! Them chicks stayed on your case, huh?"

"You better believe it! Not only that, when I first cut into the broad, at a party on the 15th floor of my hotel, I couldn't believe she was into too much.

"But there was something about her, some kinda flavor. She had class, that's what it was—class! She wasn't outrageously fine or anything, but she had this manner about her, like an antique table or somethin'.

"In addition to that, if that wasn't enough, she had so many names and titles stuck to her ass that it took the dude who introduced us, a lawd or somethin' himself, five minutes to mumble and ripple through all of 'em. I could never recall all the names, so right from the git, I wound up callin' her Suzy."

Bam and Baby June, the neighborhood junkie-wolves trotted past, looking back over their shoulders.

"Wonder what them fools done stole this time?"

"Or on they way to steal."

"Ain't no tellin', man, ain't no tellin'."

Chico Daddy shussed the side talk. "Go 'head, Buddha, what happened then?"

Chester, slightly tipsy, pulled another cigarette out and, accepting a light, smoked it without using his holder.

"Within a month after me 'n the Contessa hooked up, funny how I caught her. One minute we were in a room full of people, discussin' international bullshit in six or seven languages, next minute we was off in the library, or somewhere, standin' behind some heavy drapes and I had shot about three yards o' tongue off into her jibbs.

"Just one of those love at first sight thangs, I guess. Anyway, we got off into it. Believe me, lil' brothers, it was heavy, heavy drippin' drama.

"I bought me and the Contessa matchin' Ferraris to buzz around in. I knew, if push came to shove, we could fall back on her dough, and we were taking holidays on the Greek islands and swimmin' around Capri 'n shit. You know what I mean? Livin' that jetset lifestyle to the Max.

"I found out how easily money can slip through your fingers. I checked my accounts one day and discovered I was down to a couple hundred grand, but it didn't really matter 'cause I knew the Contessa had coins. So we kept on partyin' hearty. Nothin' mattered but that sweet life. The Contessa called it 'La Dol-che Vi-da.'

"I think I can give that so-called 'sweet life" and the Contessa credit for takin' me off into heavy drugs."

"We didn't know you was a hype, Buddha?"

"Yeahhh, I was one, for damned near five years. I had gotten onto a fast track with Suzy and one night, probably

21

for lack of anything else to do, we stuck some hyperdermic needles off into our veins and the next thing I knew, both of us had monkeys on our backs.

"I'd hate to try to guess how much of that H I'd sold in gay Paree finally wound up in my own veins. Talk about poetic justice!

"I tried to kick, a whole bunch of times, in fancy Swiss sanitariums 'n what not, you know, where rich white folks go when they want to get their heads straightened out. Nothin' worked. Number one, the Contessa was hooked and didn't give a damn and, number two, I was just weak.

"Everytime she shot up, I shot up too. By this time my money was startin' to get funny and to beat it all, I found out the Contessa was PO'!"

"She was broke?!" BoBo shot in.

"Nawww, the bitch was po', po', po'—like poverty stricken, like us. She had been drifting around for years on credit cards and her family fame 'n connections. She was po'.

"And if that wasn't bad enough, me being hooked and her being po', I found myself in love with her ass.

"In lovvvvvve, lil' brothers! Can y'all dig where I'm comin' from?!"

He leaned closely into Billy Woods' face, blowing wine fumes, gesturing extravagantly. "In fuckin' love! We had a long way to go before we'd have to start worryin' about where the next fix was comin' from, you dig?

"I had enough dough to keep us from becomin' a Bam 'n Baby June, for a while anyway. But we was going down like the Titanic. And I couldn't cut her loose 'cause I was in love with her."

The second floor window socked open again. Josie leaned out unsteadily, her hair in curlers, cold cream smeared on her face, drunk.

"Awright! You lyin' ass sonofabitch! You wanna stay

down there tellin' lies to them lil' simple-assed punks all night, huh?! That's all you wanna do! Sit round on yo' lardass, tellin' them got damned fictitious ass stories!''

Josie clutched sheets of paper in each hand as she screamed, the whole effect of her in the window both comical and tragic.

Chester sprang up from the steps, tilting slightly, panic showing.

"Josie, what the hell are you doin'?! Josie?!"

"And gotdamit! If you ain't tellin' lies, you writin' 'em! Here! Why donchu read some o' this shit to 'em! Since they so innerested in all that shit you spoutin' off!"

She flung handful after handful of handwritten manuscript out the window. The sheets of paper drifting down in the heavy night air like square flying birds, followed by shirts, suits, shoes, hats and four slow, fluttering, polka dot ascots.

"Maybe one o' them young fools will give you a place to sleep 'cause you sho' as hell ain't gon' lay up here behind me no mo' with yo' worthless, shiftless, lazy ass!"

Chester shook his fists at her, his panic replaced by rage.

"Josie! Goddamn yo' soul to hell! I told you not to ever touch my stuff!"

He lurched up the steps. The Afro-Lords, suddenly shocked out of their fairy tale groove, made a half-drunken game out of scrambling for the loose sheets of paper. Billy Woods and BoBo decked themselves out in Chester's cast off clothing.

"What the hell is it?!"

"Dig this! All the pages are numbered."

"What the fuck is it?"

"Mannnn, you dudes ain't got a bit o' couth! It's a play, Chicago Daddy, a play, can't you read?"

The Afro-Lords followed the pages, collected them, brought them together under the light of a street lamp.

23

"Here's the title, 'The Great Lawd Buddha, by Chester L. Simmons'."

"Damn! I never knew Buddha's whole name."

They ignored the serious sounds of the loud argument going on upstairs as they put the pages into numerical order.

The unmistakable sound of a pistol shot, and then five more, in slow succession, punched through the air.

The Afro-Lords, frozen in place by the first shot, stood looking sadly up to the second floor window, Chester's hats, suit coats and ascots hanging loosely on their slender shoulders.

The street had been relatively quiet, except for the rumble of the "El" train in the distance, and the million miscellaneous sounds of the ghetto, *hmmmmm thrummmmm-throbbbbbb*, was suddenly alive. The Lords scrambled to get the rest of the sheets together. Neighbors peeked cautiously out of their windows, and just as suddenly, as if by spontaneous combustion, congregated in front of Chester L. Simmons' building.

They buzzed around, gossipping, speculating, designing rumors that would fit their theories, stared at the Afro-Lords in their haphazard Chester L. Simmons garments as though they were freaks.

The bantustans law-keepers arrived, pistols drawn, four carloads full, ready to kill.

"Awright here! Everybody move aside! Clear the way here!"

They invaded the building, cautiously. And came out minutes later with Chester L. Simmons, handcuffed. The Afro-Lords waved sheets of paper at him as he was led away to a squad car.

"We got yo' play, Buddha!" Billy Woods shouted to him. "We got yo' play!"

The police reacted as though a new style riot was on the

verge of happenin', a few of them backing toward their cars with drawn guns.

"Awright now! Clear the streets! Excitement's over! Move along now and we won't have any trouble!"

The people laughed sarcastically at the white police fear and strolled away. The Afro-Lords shuffled into the hallway of the building next door. A few minutes later, two ambulance attendants arrived and brought out a cold, horseplaid blanket filled with Heatwaves' curves.

After the ambulance left, the Lords wandered in a daze, back over onto the steps. They sat there, silently putting Chester L. Simmons' play together, passing each page to Billy Woods, who read aloud as the pages were passed to him.

"Is that all, that the last page?"

"That's all we got."

Billy Woods nodded his head sadly, from side to side, and announced to the group, "Ain't no endin' to it. It ain't got no endin'."

Chapter 2

Chester L. Simmons, alias the Great Lawd Buddha, stood off by himself in a corner of the exercise yard, warming his cold bones in the bright autumn sun and reading a letter from his son, Chester, Jr. He smiled at Chester, Jr.'s description of his second grandchild, "a rubber-faced brown bouncer of a baby boy."

The Great Lawd finished the letter finally, tilted his face up toward the sun, slightly slanted eyes closed, soaking in the warmth. Life in the joint wasn't so bad, he rationalized for a moment, the sun's rays tripping him out, not if you had three squares a day, few hassles, and a chance to write as much as you wanted.

He slowly lowered his head, his prison-issued baseball cap shrouding his face with shadows. No, he scratched his earlier thought. No, that's not right, being in jail is pure hell.

He looked out across the yard, his eyes sweeping across a panorama of misery, self-hate, dumb rage, hostility,

27

inhumane cruelty and human degradation. Chester L. Simmons, the Great Lawd Buddha, Mississippian, Black brotherman, poet, dramatist, world spieler, artist, speculator, murderer.

His thoughts twisted away from the snake pit scene in front of him, back in time, to his life with Josie "Heatwave" Scott, the one-time apple of his eye, the lady who made him blow his cool, six times into her gorgeous body with a German Luger.

Why did it have to be Josie? Why Josie? he'd asked himself a few dozen profound times, behind a terrible day under a sadistic guard, or after a dismal night, dreaming of the flavor of her body's aromas, the warmth of her eyes, the shape of her nose, her lush mouth, her neck, her gorgeous titties, her navel, her rainbow hips, the grizzled sporran between her thighs, her magnificent ass, thoughts that took him beyond momentary unpleasantries, like doing twenty to life.

But, life being what it is, he philosophized, it had to be Josie. Sigghhh. C'est la vie.

He plunged his hands deeper into his pockets, the anguish of five thousand hours of remose tilting his face back up into the sun, seeking warmth, oblivion from haunted memories. They were on him before he was aware of their presence.· "Whass happenin', bruh Buddha?" the boldest of the trio asked.

He pinned all three evenly. Tough, hip, literate young Black captives. into books 'n politics. Good.

"Nothin' to it, lil' brothers, a baby could do it."

He leaned against the cement wall at his back and crossed his legs. Which one would pop the question? They always had something to ask, something they wanted to know. "Buddha, what's this shit we hear 'bout you being declared a white man in South Africa?" Marcus the bank robber asked point blank and squatted in place to hear the full story.

"Ohh, that," Buddha super-casually tossed off and squatted·himself down slowly into his Sumo wrestling rest stance, glad to talk a lil' stuff to open minds.

"That, hah hah, that was the result of a most weird set of circumstances, most weird. If I could possibly bum a cigarette from one of you golden brothers, I would be most happy to run the whole thing down to you."

Marcus held his pack out to him immediately, pleased to be able to supply the bribe. One could never tell; one day, it might be candy, one day a lil' powdered nutmeg to snort, or snuff or cocaine, but most often, just a few cigarettes.

"It all started after I had to make my European break, behind my heroin sting. I told you all about that, didn't I? Being hounded by those Algerian mafia dudes over that kilo I çopped?"

The three men nodded solemnly, one of their favorite dramas.

"Okay, there I was, once again, on a freighter, I used to go a lotta places on freighters, this time as a common swabbie. I had stolen or traded for a Malay seaman's documents who looked like me, on the way to wherever the brute that I was treadin' water on was headed.

"Now, why we had to wind up in Capetown, South Africa is something that only God above and the captain of the sleazy bitch we was sailin' on could answer. Cape-town, South Afri-ca," he enunciated syllable by syllable, as though grinding his teeth on something bitter.

"I'll never know why, what demonic force caused me to jump ship in a place like that, but I did. In many ways it was unequivocally one of the grooviest Black places I've ever been in this world. I mean, like sho' nuff groovy gut bucket Black. Everybody after white, that is to say, the so called colored, Cape Malays, Indians, Zulus, Xosas, Basutos, Pondos, everybody but white helped everybody else.

"I had some dudes help put together all the documents I needed, just to walk the streets. Them crazy Boers had one of the most insane pass systems the world has ever seen, put together by one of our country's great computer companies. Dig it?

"I had people feed me (and lawd knows they didn't have much), pass me around like I was a cookie that might crumble up in their hands," his voice rumbled dramatically. "Because I was a soul brother from the U-nited States who had decided, they thought, to stay with them in their locations, share their oppression and their fight for liberation. Beautiful people, gentlemen, beautiful people, carved out of love."

He accepted another cigarette, chain fashion, and carried on, caught up by his story.

"I had three families slip me around in their location for two weeks, just ahead of the state police, the Gestapo is really what they were. Now dig it! I feel I must elaborate on this point because it is most important. I was a potentially dangerous, slick minded U-nited States nigger who had obviously jumped ship for subversive reasons, and was known to do my share of dirt...that is, if the whole truth be known."

Donnel, Marcus and Brian all held their hands out to be slapped, their common sense of wrong doing embroidered, for them, in a way that they had never heard it before.

"The South African police, brothermen," he continued more slowly, in a heavier tone. "The South African police could bring pee to a chump's eyes, if they caught you gettin' down wrong, missin' a step, or doin' any such shit as they could misconstrue as being against their regime.

"And there I was: young, foolish, wild, so crazy that I didn't even know why I had jumped ship. Well, the rats, no women and lousy food may have been contributing factors. Some of the militant brothers thought I had come over secretly as a Black Che Guevara, but actually, that wasn't it at all.

"It was just stupidity what done it. Nobody had ever really told me about the racial set up, really. Nobody had told me that the Afrikkaners discriminated against everybody, even they own mommas."

The trio laughed indulgently, pulling their collars up against the deepening chill.

"Yeahhh, that's right! Even they own mommas! There was a case while I was there, of a police inspector who caught his momma with the yardboy and was so outraged that he had the Racial Classification Board declare his momma one piece nigger, shifted her away from him, had the Re-Classification Board bypass him and kept on livin' happily ever after with his snow white wife. Helluva country, gentlemen! I'm tellin' ya the nachul bone truth! Helluva country!"

Marcus nodded in serious agreement, his reading having covered the South African Cancer.

"After a bit, some of the dudes who were looking out for me, at the risk of their lives, helped get me a gig, underground, down in the diamond mines."

"Diamond mines?!" Donnell showed the gold caps on his teeth in surprise.

"That's what you heard, amigo, diamonds! Diamonds!" The Great Lawd Buddha licked his lips and sparkled his eyes in the oblique rays of the setting sun, caricaturing greed.

"Every morning at 4:30 a.m. we slaves—yeahhh, that's just about what we were too, slaves, makin' so little a day, when you think about how much income we were makin' for the Baas, translated meaning Boss.

"But actually goin' deeper than that, cause they had a system based on that Baas thing, called Baaskap or Baaskamf or somethin' like that, that was supposed to keep everybody unwhite underground for the rest of their lives, and after they died, they'd get left there, underground."

Marcus jammed his hands deeper into his blue denim jacket pockets and scowled at the wall above Buddha's head.

"Sounds like Miss'ssippi, or New Yawk, don't it?"

"Really!" Donnel affirmed, quietly slapping Buddha's outstretched hand.

"But actually it was worse than that. Much worse. At any rate, I'm down underneath the ground, siftin' diamonds up big as your fist, turning each 'n every one into the Baas, til one day my treacherous U-nited States nigger mind started shootin' off sparks.

"I knew that some of the dudes managed to get away with a few tiny, industrial type gems every month. What I wanted to do was cop some authentic stones.

"So, I got on my job. It was really hard for a while, to get my organization together. I mean, like a few of the more unsophisticated African brothers didn't even feel that it was right to steal from the Baas."

"Buddha! You got to be jivin'!"

"I wouldn't jive you, youngblood," he answered, dead pan under his cap.

"But you see, their minds were formed in a tribal mold, they didn't think it was right to steal from *anybody*, and to lots of 'em, despite the fact that they suffered under him, the white man was still a human being.

"Deep, huh? Probably one of the main reasons why all those Black folks over there haven't formed a wall and just pushed the sucker into the sea. Anyway, after a bit, I escaped from the mines . . ."

"Escaped?" Brian exclaimed.

"Uhhh huhhnnn, E-scaped. You see, at that time, you signed a 'contract' for two years and the only way you could break it was to E-scape. I escaped and became a fence for the dudes I had organized in the mines.

"My thang went a lil' bit like this: I'd pay about 25 dollars for a helluva gem, 50, U.S. rates, for a fantastic gem and 100, at least, for one of those overwhelming pinkie rings that you sometimes see on the small fingers of eminent homos and stark ravin' rich Harlem pimps. I moved fast, bought everything that I could get my hands on, dealt with a rich ol' unscrupulous diamond merchant who had an interest in the mines that the stones were being ripped off from. He really had a number goin'. He couldn't lose for winnin', makin' grand theft coins from both ends.

"You dudes ever see a diamond merchant?"

The three men, mechanically, nodded no in unison.

"Well, take my word for it, they, 'long with the diamond cutters, are weird lookin' lil' bitty dudes. They all got pointed heads, usually bald, and don't have no emotion whatsoever and would do anything for diamonds. Love them diamonds.

"The dude I was dealin' with, tryin' to pull a super grand stake together, in order to split the scene, tried to have me arrested a couple times, and when that didn't work, I got word of what was goin' down through the grapevine, tried to have me assassinated. All he cared about was diamonds, period."

He stood up to stretch his legs and eased back down into position, belly hanging over his belt, Sumo style.

"Anyway, within two months or so, I had scrounged up 'bout $600,000 worth o' gems, some really good 'n some pretty bad, and I was ready to hat up. But, as lady luck would have it, the night before I got ready to split, I was leavin' a Xosa lady's crib, a really too fine sister named Christa, at 12:30 a.m. and got picked up for a pass violation, and that's when the doodoo hit the propeller."

Buddha paused to exchange solemn nods with six members of a Chicano group to whom he had given a Third World

33

talk to, the day before.

"Yeahhh, it sho' nuff hit the fan," he continued. "Number one, the Gestapo must have spent three or four months grillin' me, tryin' to make me tell them who the Baas was, behind my organization. The more I told them that I was, the less they believed me.

"Finally, it dawned on one of those superduper crackers that I was the Baas. Now that really twisted their lil' ol' hate filled minds around. *Me*, Chester L. Simmons from Miss'ssippi, one of their sister states, had actually been the brains behind some grand theft action. It was too much for them!

"Now what they did, some beaurocrat in the Racial Determination section, was this: since it was obvious that no Black man could possibly have schemed at such a level, then I must be a white man, a member of the Baasdom."

"Wowww! Talk about goin' through some changes," Marcus burst out, eyes digging the Great Lawd.

"Changes, you say? Uhh huh, as good a word for it as you could use. What was happenin', aside from all the money I was usin' to bribe everybody and his brother with, was this: On the socio-political propaganda side, the authorities didn't want any kind of word to leak out, officially, about my gettin' past the diamond mine check system. Me, a Black brother! I mean, like, after all, that would give a lot o' people big ideas. So, therefore, in that typical iron-headed way they had of doin' things, they had me declared a white man. Can you git ready for that?"

"You a bad dude, Buddha," Donnell solemnly assured him.

"But this time I'd been in the slams, in solitary, for about six months. But my money was workin' for me. I managed to stick coins to the Prime Minister's uncle even. Anything to get out.

"Now, dig it, young brothers, I'll tell you the truth. If I'm lyin', I hope God'll strike me dead."

He paused for a cigarette and a light.

"I don't know who really decided that the best thing to do was deport me, but I sho' am grateful. Aside from my bribery, they wanted to git rid of me for socio-political reasons. They didn't want a declared white man that looked kinda Black in jail, creating some weird kind of martyr for the Blacks, so they forced me to agree to a deportation scene, sort of a primitive plea bargainin' number.

"Well, heyyy, you can imagine how I felt. I would've agreed to anything to get out of that place. Anything!"

"Right on!" Brian cued in, alert to the circumstances.

"Well, you can believe they fucked me over a lil' bit before I was finally released. One day the guard would announce that I was leavin' that evenin', then turn right around and tell me to forget about it...as well as your other kinds of regular torture.

"The South African white man is a stranger to most of the rest of the human race, him and the red-necked Miss'ssippian. I don't really know what happened to them during the evolutionary process, but I do know this, a special kind of sickness settled into both of 'em hundreds of years ago and they've never been close to being healthy."

The Great Lawd Buddha pursed his lips reflectively and slowly stood, his eyes following the lazy flight of a pigeon.

Marcus, Donnel and Brian followed the direction of his eyes.

Brian, impatiently wanting to hear the end of Buddha's story before the evening lock up said, "Uhh, so they booted you out, huh?"

"In the dead of night, my friend, in the dead of night," he continued, snatching his eyes away from the pigeon's flight. "Me and three other 'undesirable aliens'. However,

35

I could say, as a history maker, that I had had the opportunity to be a Black whiteman in one of the most prejudiced white places on Mother Earth, and you can believe me, that takes some doin'.

"Awright, deported, hardshippin' and in Zambia, tryin' to shit out a few of these stones I'd stuffed away in my precious lil' body."

"You got away with some?"

"Clean as a whistle! They'd made me take some laxatives 'n shit, but years ago, in India—that's another whole story—a great Yoga man taught me how to control my bowels. I mean, like I once knew how to half shit, or fart at three different tonal levels, and a whole bunch of other things, but you know how it is if you don't practice.

"At any rate. I was home free, a pocketful of precious stones, off to trade with the Conquerin' Lion of Judah, the King of Kings, His Imperial Lawdship, Haibe Selassi himself."

"Oh wowwww."

"Yessuh! I figured that the only righteous dude I could deal with would be the Emperor of Ethiopia. I knew if anybody had any money at all, it would be him. So, off I go, to Ethiopia."

The guard on the tower station above them, concerned about lengthening shadows and the intensity of their closeness, motioned them out to the center of the yard.

Marcus scowled up at the guard. "Hey, I got a lil' home brew in my cell, y'all wanna...?"

"No sooner said than done!" Buddha agreed quickly, the last rays of the sun disappearing over the wall, chilling him to the bone.

The four of them made their way through the relays of contraband searchers, up to their tier. Marcus ushered them into his cell, as though he were receiving guests in a swank house.

"Make yourselves to home, it ain't much but it all belongs to the state."

He uncovered a potent half pint of distilled potato drippings, rubbing alcohol, iodine (for color) and the residue of several past batches, and passed it to the guest of honor.

"Oooowheeee!" Buddha exclaimed, squinching up his already squinched up eyes. "Goddamn! this shit is u-gly!"

Having given it his stamp of approval, he took another long swallow. The trio beamed around him.

"Go on, Buddha. You was in Ethiopia."

"Uh huh, sho' was. Got a fair 'n square deal on my gems from His Majesty, hung around Addis A-Gabba long enough to sock a couple crumberushers into a few ladies and departed, ten minutes ahead of three tribes of brothers intent on makin' me marry their sisters and a red hot case of ol' fashioned plague."

Donnel spilled a little of the homebrew out the side of his mouth.

"What kinda plague?"

"The bubonic plague, young suh, the bubonic plague. The kind that they used to have in Europe that would kill off half of London, or Paris or Amsterdam. The plague plague.

"But like I said, I was off. What I was goin' to do was hit off 'round the eastern coast, shoot through the upper Sudan right quick, slice through Egypt—I hadn't been to Cairo yet—whip around the edge of Libya, maybe get on back into Europe from Algeria, if everything was cool.

"As it turned out, everything was love jones, 'til I got to Algeria. Somebody had put out a contract on my body. I don't have to tell you who, and I guess it was stupid of me to be thinkin' that the Algerians who wanted my guts wouldn't check back home every now and then.

"Anyway, whilst I was dodging knives, bullets and shit

being dropped from roof tops, they had started another one of those lil' ol' funny time wars they were in the habit of havin'. I think this one was about some dude snatchin' some other dude's woman's veil off.''

"Pass it on, Donnell!" Brian reminded as he stared hypnotically into Buddha's mouth.

Buddha accepted the half empty half pint bottle and bowed while seated, supergraciously, half lit.

"I got out," he said curtly, after a quick swallow. "Are we completely cigaretteless?"

Marcus lit one and handed it to him.

"Yeahhh, I got out, fled to Casablanca, Morocco. Now that's a town for you if ever there was one! At the time I swooped in, everything went! You hear me, lil' brothers!? Everything!

"I hadn't been in town fifteen hot minutes, black in white, white on black, moppin' my face with a snow white handkerchief, when two of the most beautiful lil' girls, teenagers actually, grabbed me to lead me to their virgin mother."

The men winked across the booze and their male feelings for those scenes.

"What could I say? What could I do? I 'married' all three of 'em that weekend and settled down to a harmonious domestic life. I must hasten to add, right in through here, however, the kind of 'domestic life' I had wasn't all that domestic.

"'Within three months, I had gotten my pinky finger into the hash trade, had my big toe into the cocaine thing, and was handlin' a few choice gems. I had learned a whole lot about how to judge a stone from the ol' pointy headed diamond merchant, and the rest of me was pushed off into them French diplomat's wives, those that has a lil' somethin' to add to the family treasury.

38

"But, as usual, I got greedy. The more I had, the more I wanted. I tried to corner the hash market and the king got pissed off and kicked me out. He was usin' my hash thang as an excuse, but what he really wanted was my woman, Fatima."

The Great Lawd Buddha uncoiled himself slowly from Marcus's bunk, stood looking through the barred Gothic window, remembering.

When he spoke again, after long, moments of deep thought, his voice, a soundtrack of his experiences in life, carried the flavor of the souk, the yearning cry of te kif fiend, the smoke and intrigue of Northern Africa.

"Fatima. Fatima." He pronounced her name reverently, as though whispering into the Prophet's ear. "So beautiful, so deep and arrogant that when she walked through the streets, pin-striped tattoo-blued from her chin to her bottom lip, body shaped like a lovely Coca Cola bottle, dudes used to walk into the sides of buildings, or start prayin' right on the spot. And Aissa and Naima were just about as fine as their mother.

"So much of what was happenin' to me in those days was so mysterious, so unbelievable. Like Fatima and her daughters, for example. And I had to leave it all," he said suddenly, turning away from the window to remount the seat of honor.

"Yes, once again I had to leave it or run the risk of being drowned by the King's men in a sand dune somewhere."

"Hey Marcus! You got any black shoe polish?!" A fellow con leaned into the cell door.

Marcus frowned, nodded no and tried to wave him away, but the brother, peeking in, caught up by the expressions on everyone's face, eased in and squatted at the foot of Marcus's bunk.

Buddha, Algerian Flamenco, wavy blue sand, homebrew,

Rabat, Marrakesh, Casablanca and Fatima sizzling through his imagination, merely nodded at the addition and rapped on.

"After my expulsion, I don't know what happened to me. I became a lost man. It was as though my senses didn't work anymore, as though too much had happened. It was terrible, purely and simply terrible, my brothers.

"I became a soulless, ash splattered, piss stained, doodoo covered representative of humanity, sleeping wherever my head found itself, eatin' goat turds and rat shit, searchin' for my Self again."

The addition to the group looked from one face to the other, seeking some explanation for where they were, but receiving none, listened harder.

"If you can get into what my trip was. Here, I had been declared a white man in South Africa, managed to avoid the perils of being lynched, made it around the eastern fringe of Mamma Africa and all of a sudden, for only reasons that the Great It has an explanation for, I find myself in rags, walkin' down through Maritania, tryin' my goddamnedest to get to someplace on the west coast, to get on a freighter, or a slave ship, or somethin', headed for the Indies, at least. My luck had run out and I knew it."

He turned the bottle up and sipped delicately, as though it were his by reason of possession. No one bothered to correct him.

"I still had a diamond big enough to constipate an elephant in my rags, but I was savin' that for the finale, for my grand exit from Africa. What I had in mind to do was drop it in the Atlantic, a hardened tear for the souls of all our brothers 'n sisters who had jumped, been pushed, or had in some way wound up being shark's grub for a few hundred years, durin' the black human being trade."

Marcus, an Our-storian, looked at the Great Lawd Buddha with a tearful gleam in his eye, the homebrew almost pushing

40

it out.

"In Africa, amongst the religious people, you always pour what they call a libation to the Great It, on every occasion. That's what I had planned to do. But, as usual, Miss Fate spread her tricky fingers all over my plans.

"I wouldn't even attempt to try to take you dudes through all the super-natural trips, all the days and nights of starvation, both physical and spiritual, the times I was lost amongst people who thought I was a god, or a dog, all of the moments of intense ecstacy and profound sadness I experienced durin' my two year walk."

"two year *walk*?!" the newcomer exclaimed.

"Shut up, Amos," Brian said quietly.

"Yeahhh, two years I walked." Buddha favored him with a wise, hip, old glance. "From the outskirts of Casablanca, through what they used to call the Spanish Sahara, Mauritania, Senegal, Guinea, Liberia, the Ivory Coast, on into Ghana.

"Now strangely enough, for some reason, by the time I made it to Ghana, my mind seemed to clear itself, to come alive again. All of a sudden it seemed that I was amongst my people. Can y'all get into where I'm comin' from?"

His audience nodded yes, yes, yes, yes.

"I don't know what it was, really. Maybe it was that cup of twenty-five day old palm wine a sister on the fringes of Accra laid on me, or the words of an American blood who spoke to me, or whatever, but one thing was certain, I was back in the world.

"Naturally, I wound up dealin' with the slickest motherfuckers in six countries for this stone I had. Got a decent price for it too, went out and copped some hip kente cloth robes, partied a lil' bit, and the next thing I know, the Asantehene of the Ashanti people is requestin' the pleasure of my appearance.

41

"The Asantehene! If y'all don't know who he is, I can't begin to tell you. All I can say is this! When the Asantehene wants you, you wind up being where he wants you. He's sort of like part God and part African.

"So there I am, in a huge room with the Asantehene and his linguist. That's the dude who does all his rappin' for him.

"The Asantehene is sitting on a golden throne, with gold strands of thread hangin' down over his face, a couple gold nuggets weighin' his fingers down, gold woven all into his robes. Gold, dammit! Everywhere! And the linguist, a hip lil' ol' brother, about 16 years older than kola nuts, is rappin' to me, tellin' me that the Asantehene wants me to find the Golden Stool for him.

"He wants me, you dig?! Chester L. Simmons, to find the Golden Stool for him. I almost shat granola crumbs when I heard that. Why me?

"And then the Asantehene spoke, or rather threw his voice from over in a corner. Must've been a ventriloquist. Had a voice like a bass conga drum.

" 'I have followed your movement around the outer edges of our continent, I know of your spiritual battles, what you have suffered and overcome,' he says to me in letter perfect, high-toned English. 'And it is for these reasons, and many deeper ones, that I ask you to find the soul of my nation.'

"Behind that he didn't say another mumblin' word, he just sat there, just as cool and serene as you please. The linguist held a medium sized leather pouch out to me and I crawled out on my hands and knees, the way I'd crawled in. I mean, like that's the way you came to the Asantehene.

"Once I got outside, about five blocks from the palace, I opened the strings to the pouch and discovered it was filled with gold dust. Gold dust! I was shitless speechless. It was like...it was like the Great It had asked you to find his favorite pillow and paid you out front for it.

42

"Now the thing was, I couldn't say anything to anybody because nobody was supposed to know that the Stool was missin'. I mean, like if the Stool was known to be missin', the symbolic heart of the nation, people would start dyin' off, out of sadness or whatever, ten thousand natural catastrophes would occur, in addition to the fact that the Asantehene would be lynched in 46 different ways, along with every member of his family, and his name would be recited forever, as the dude who blew the Stool. You talk about a motherfucker in serious trouble! I ain't talkin' 'bout him, I'm talkin' about me!

"If I succeeded in recoverin' the Stool, no one but the Asantehene and his linguist would know about it. If I didn't recover the Stool, my ass would be in a sling, six feet under, and no one would know about that either. I mean, it be a thang, like you don't be failin' when the Asantehene puts you on your job.

"I was so shook up that I went off and drank pink gin for a week, tryin' to find the vision for what I was supposed to be doin'."

He turned the corner of the bottle up and killed it, so into his story that he had forgotten about the other people in the cell.

"Oooopps, sorry 'bout that!" he apologized graciously.

"Fuck that, man! Go on, what happened?" Marcus shot in.

"Well, once I got my head together, I started gettin' the kind of logical vibes I needed. By the process of elimination, I figured out certain things.

"Number one, no Asanti would be caught dead, or alive with the Stool, their...uhhh...sensibilities just wouldn't know how to deal with it. It would be like havin' God's Ghost locked up in a closet.

"I was pretty certain that none of the other tribal groups had copped the Stool because if they had, hah hah hah, well,

43

if they had, they would've had a war on their hands that would've been guaranteed annihilation for everybody, forever. And ever.

"Okay, havin' gone up 'n down and in 'n out in my head, who could I settle on that would be insensitive enough, disrespectful enough, vicious enough, and cold blooded enough to rip off the soul of a nation?"

"The white boy!" Brian called out.

The Great Lawd Buddha leaned over unsteadily, the potato drippings singing in his skull, to slap Brian's palm with a sauve stroke.

"Right! A foreigner! Now I really had a problem. The English, currently in power at the time, didn't dig me being in the country in the first place and if I made too many wrong moves, my ass was gon' be in another sling, so I had to proceed quietly."

A fellow inmate's sudden screaming on the tier below them sliced through Buddha's monologue. They all tensed up. They knew the sound well. Someone receiving a Dear John letter or suddenly being overcome by the pressure of the cage surrounding him, or from a thousand other prisoned feelings, had gone insane.

The man, his lungs suddenly lined with steel, screamed until the keepers made their immediate appearance, billy clubs and gas guns at the ready, prepared to beat, gas and drag him off to the Hole, for "rehabilitation."

Buddha accepted another cigarette, his hands shaking slightly. It was important to go on, to fight the bad vibes.

"As we all know," he continued, "money talks, all kinds o' money. So, that's what I put to work for me. That, and my game.

"It took me something like two months to find out how many, which and where, foreign archeological expeditions had been or was diggin'. I had cornered things down to that.

44

Since no one had ever seen the Stool, other than the Asantehene, I figured that some fool archeologists, rapin' the country like they was doin' in those days, had stumbled across the piece and was definitely keepin' it cool 'til they got it out of the country.

"Usin' the elimination process again, I sifted the expeditions, a French group, an Italian group, a Portuguese group, of all things, and about eight English groups, naturally.

"Gentlemen, you talkin' 'bout a dude earnin' his dust! I sho' 'nuff earned mine that year. I wheeled and dealed my way to the Stool, all boxed and on its way to Rome, two days before the S.S. Aida sailed. What I did was this: I found out that the Italians had stumbled across the Stool, which was buried, had lied to the English colonial-master guys about what they had found, and was gettin' ready to arreviderchi.

"Awright. Playin' the game, I managed to slip work in to the H.E.I.C., Head Englishman in Charge. Naturally, he's severely pissed off. I mean, like they were gonna put all the dagos in jail 'n shit, but what he was really super happy about was gettin' his grubby hands on the Stool!

"As y'all know, the goddamned English had fought a war with the Ashanti over the Stool years back, so they really felt groovy about gettin' their hands on something that they'd fought like dogs for. But heyyy, this *is* the Great Lawd Buddha, right?!"

"Right on, Buddha! Right on!" Brian yelled, oblivious to his surroundings.

"Yessuh. So what I did, with about eight of the most nerviest Ashanti dudes you ever thought about hearin' about, was perform the most perfectly executed rip off in the history of the country.

"One of the dudes who helped me rip off the Stool later became a top dog in the government, after Ghana became

45

independent. The dudes who was in on it, incidentally, refused to be paid. My con to them was—you dig?—'I want you all to help me pull off a fantastic, unreal, daylight holdup on the English.' That's all I had to say to those dudes, that's all, that we were goin' to embarrass the English so bad that they would be walkin' 'round with red faces for days.

"And that's what we did. I organized a tribal festival that involved the Asantehene, with his connivance, of course. And while he's layin' his blessin' on the building the festival revolved around, with the Duke 'n Duchess, the King's representatives in attendance—they just happened to be in town, hah hah hah—this is what we did: At the high point of things, my hip Ashanti buddies eased off with the Stool on their shoulders, in a crate, singin' 'n drummin' 'n shit, in the middle of about fifty 'leven million fellow tribesmen.

I'll never know for certain, but I think, I say, I think the English knew what we goin' down but they couldn't scream 'Hay, bring that bloody Stool back!' 'Cause they couldn't admit they had it, not with all those brothers out there.

"On the other hand, the Asantehene couldn't admit that he was stealin' it back, 'cause he was never supposed to have lost it in the first place. We wound up with what you might call an impasse.

"Three days after the grand theft, the Asantehene called me in again, laid another bag o' dust on me, without sayin' nary a word. Two days after that, the English 'advised' me to get on.

"Or, as I remember the way the young blond stud put it, 'UHHH, Simmons, we should like to see you depart on the next scheduled ship from the area.'

"When's that, I asked.

"'This afternoon', he told me, and didn't blink once.

"So, once again, there I was, orphaned in the world." He stood and stretched. "Yeahhh, orphaned in the world."

He bowed to the men in the call, as though he were a Mandarin lord, and strolled onto the tier passageway, heading for his own cell, and the horrors awakened within himself, from a couple hours of storytelling.

"Buddha?!" Marcus called to him as he made his suave exit.

He turned, a cell away, a quizzical expression on his Benin-Mao shaped face.

"Buddha, you ever think about doin' your autobiography?"

Buddha gave him a cold smile. "Yeah, I did once, it got all messed up, that's why I'm in here."

Marcus looked down at the floor helplessly, and back up to see Buddha disappear into his own cell, ready for the evening lock up.

Buddha buttoned the top button of his rough, heavy woolen pajamas, pulled his blankets up under his chin, laced his hands behind his head and gazed through the barred cell window at the bristling stars beyond. He shivered slightly, not from actual cold, but from the thought of it. Never could stand the cold too well, always loved the warmth more.

He looked away from the squared off picture of the bright moon and stars, over to his writing table, a small wooden version of a card table, ignoring the loud, snuffly noises of his cellmate, Ranklin C. Jones, a hold-up man, dreaming on his bunk against the opposite wall.

Buddha lay wide awake, filtering the hundreds of midnight jailhouse sounds through his consciousness; the snoring, whispered escape plans, blues hummers, coughers, the squealings of homosexual assaults, the groans and grunts of homosexual relations; the dazzling array of mad sounds that could only come from caged men.

He sat up on the side of his bunk, feeling restless, feeling the urge to write. He smiled at the thought as he pulled the

47

table across the narrow distance to his knees, draped his blankets over his shoulders and sat, alternately staring through the window and down at the notebook and pencils on the table in front of him.

He finally opened the notebook, frowned at the smudge marks on the first five pages, a legacy of Ranklin C. Jones's surreptitious interest, and read up to where he had stopped writing the night before.

"I think the geography book is what carried me off into fantasia, in the beginning."

He picked up one of the pencils beside the notebook, checked the point in the bright glare of the moonshine, no need for the tension lamp, and began to write, the moon and stars seeming to offer more light with the formation of each word. "How could I *not* be carried off, in the Beginning, down there in the racial swamp?"

He stirred his pencil around in mid-air for a few seconds, mentally reviewing the six lynchings he had watched from a distance during his boyhood, and the far more numerous ones he had managed to escape from, acting 'uppity' in Miss'ssippi, Amerikka.

"Yes, it was the geography book that carried me off," he continued, "reading about far away places and other kinds of people. Anything would have done it," he wrote. "Anything at all, a soft word, a gentle look, electric lights, an indoor toilet, maybe the hooting of a midnight flyer. But it was none of these, it was the geography book."

Settling into a stride, he crossed his ankles and pulled the blankets tighter around his shoulders.

"God only knows how I came across the damned thing, if my memory serves me correctly, we only had twelve books in our whole big one room schoolhouse and none of them had a range of thought beyond Lil' Black Sambo, the Family in the Cotton Fields and such like, but one day, as such things do happen...there it is...tattered, battered and readable, with pictures yet.

"I can recall even now, oh so clearly, how pissed I was to come to the African section of the book and find all the people looking so black and strange. But that was many years ago, thank God! And I've since developed a more sophisticated view of Blackness."

He paused, smiling, as he watched Ranklin C. Jones moan and sensually rub his testicles.

"Everything was strange in that book, the people, the words (it took me quite awhile to understand some of them, geopolitics, for example), the names, all of it! That is, until I began to make my own framework for all of it.

"I find myself constantly referring to something I call the Beginning.

"For want of a better word, I guess I'll have to stay there, for a few emotional beats, before I go on to the upper levels of purgatory.

"The strong, always tired, black dirt working robots, who happened to be my parents, and all of the relatives who looked and acted pretty much as they did, were not the Beginning, nor was the clapboard shack with the old newspapers wadded into the cracks, nor was the white man who had the power of life and death over us.

"No, it was the aroma of places I'd never smelled, the look in a pair of eyes I'd never seen, the urge to wander around inside my soul. That was the Beginning.

"Once released from my extended bondage by the power of the book, I wandered around the world, doing the undoable. I slept with the white women, blondes, in defiance of all of Miss'ssippi's rule. I climbed Fujiyama, looked the sacred leopard on the top of Kilimanjaro in the eyes, ran with the bulls of Pamplona, went off into fern-coated shacks with Polynesian goddesses, who nursed me through tropical

49

fevers, killed lions and elephants for the favor of the hand of the Oba's youngest daughter. I emigrated to old China on a dilapidated freighter, and found myself on the southside of Chicago in the middle of the winter time.

"But what did it matter? After I found that the only thing I had to do was open up a dozen, a hundred, a thousand other books, that would sweep me away just as quickly."

A heavy blanket of clouds oozed across the moon's face, temporarily darkening his effort. He waited impatiently for it to pass, aware once again of the richness of night noises in the pen. Somebody typing on the tier below. Must be Kwendi.

Yeah, that would be him. Young stud never sleeps it seems, with all that revolutionary stuff on his mind, but who am I to talk about people not sleeping?

The clouds passed, leaving him blinded by the re-emergence of the moonlight.

"Leaving Miss'ssippi three steps ahead of the lynch mob, and working, bumming, conning, doing whatever else necessary to make life happen was a great book.

"I wish I had the nerve to try and remember all of it. Starving almost to death in a hermit's shack down in Cairo, Illinois. Why Cairo, Illinois? my imagination said to me. Why not Cairo, Egypt? And I was off. The one room shack became a fifty room hashish den, owned by a funky but ptolemic aristocrat.

"It's a very strange thing to admit to yourself, after so long, that you are a liar. But I wonder about me, specifically me, on this score. Have I really been a liar all these years, or a geography teacher?"

He frowned at the sound of the toilet being flushed in the next cell.

"What does it really matter? After all is said and done about what you are, someone once said, it's what you have done with what you are. And what was I before I was tamed? Had the iron doors slammed behind me and the key thrown away?'' The moon glared at the fierce smile he turned up to it. "What was I? A question that not many men as wise as myself would even attempt to deal with."

He paused, on the verge of writing a lie, before going on with the truth.

"I was a conning, cunning, scheming, dreaming, shrewd, slick, conniving beast, a miniature dinosaur with a huge brain, a lecher, a consummate player I was—at one time, the hippest of the hip."

He had to stop writing for a moment, to cool out the gush of egotism he felt rising within himself.

"Yes, at one time, I was me, a supersonic, geopolitical macman. There've been times when I've found myself flashing across the face of the planet, taking those who could come with me, on the strength of a name, Yemen, Jakarta, Hunza, Moeshoeshoe, Lhasa, Huatabampo, Mundina ...God! Whatever happened to Mundina? Yes, if not the name of a place, the name of a woman, or her perfume, or the shape of her ear lobe.

"I was that, a lover of the lives of the women who thought that the greatest gift they had to offer was their bodies, and all I really wanted, in most cases, was their stories."

The sour-sweet memory of "Heatwave" set off a dull, achy feeling around the region of his heart.

"The ladies of my summer in life, the Circassians, the Navajos, the hundreds of hours of glamorous sorrow I suffered, taking my grizzled lovebone into and out of their holy slits, putting my mind into the position of being given something more precious than all the cunt they could possibly lay on me.

"Back and forth I've gone, across these United States, from east to west, from north to south, tripping into Mexican villages, near Detroit, or raiding the striped tents of rival Beduins, because that's what the book said one should do, just this side of the Golden Gate Bridge.

"The moments I've had, the exquisite flavors of ten thousand make-do stews in a thousand hobo jungles, the glistening stories recited by shattered men with hearts of tempered steel, the little campfires, the rivers of cheap wine."

He let the pencil slip out of his fingers and leaned back against the wall, wishing he had a cigarette. Maybe bruh Rank has one.

He peered across at Ranklin C. Jones, at the silly smile slicing his brown face in dreamland—probably dreaming of Pam Grier's titties—and checked out the area surrounding him and spotted a half smoked cigar in a jar lid under the edge of his bunk.

Oh well, what the hell.

He skirted the edge of his table, stooped for the half done stogie, found a match and lit up, frowning from the first puff. Guess beggars can't be choosy.

He remounted his seat behind the table, the smoke from the cheap cigar held down too long giving him a cheap high.

He looked closely at the last words he had written. Rivers of wine, rivers of wine, days and nights of frustration, illness, suffering, a lifetime of dismal failure.

"How hard it is to tell the truth. A lifetime of failure. To be able, after all these years, to say that. To say that I've never been to Europe, Africa, Asia, or any other fuckin' place outside my country 'tis of thee."

He dropped the smoldering cigar butt on the floor, feeling angry with himself.

"Made it up as I went along, that's what I did. I made it all up. The windblown feasts on the Mongolian steppers with kurdish tribesmen, here's yogurt in your eye!

"The Japanese Penis Worshipping Society, Chester L. Simmons, aka the Great Lawd Buddha, President. Down, girls, down! The voudoun thang in Papa Doc's Haiti, Ogun's ride on my head, my career as a nudist photographer on the French Rivera, the kisses I exchanged with the princesses of twelve nations, including that coldblooded young English bitch who loved horses more than she liked men!

"The rackets, the games, the schemes, the hustles. All lies! all lies!"

He looked up, surprised to see the sky streaked by the first signs of another day, in this instance, Thursday. But no matter, they were all the same in the joint. He hurried on, writing as though the full day would destroy everything he had written.

"My life has been one glorified lie, from Beginning to End. A lie that deviated from time to time but still remained a life. Or maybe I should put it another way: Where other men have habitually told the truth and lied sometimes, I have always lied and told the truth as seldom as possible. For me, a lie."

"What's happenin', Buddhaman?" Ranklin yawned across at him, ending his story for the moment.

Buddha nodded his head neutrally, plastering his opaque look on.

"You been writin' all night again?"

"That's right, brother, all night long."

Ranklin stepped onto the floor gingerly, tiptoed over to the unenclosed stool to relieve his bladder.

"Mannnn, I don't see how you do it, I have a helluva time tryin' to scribble my woman a few lines every now 'n then."

Buddha smiled and, with the rest of the stirring inmates, prepared to deal with another jailhouse day, before the breakfast gong.

"Buddha?" The guard called to him through the bars.

53

"Yeah, what can I do for you, Smitty?" Buddha turned to him casually, folding his blankets on his bunk, looking forward already to the nap he would steal later in the day.

"Warden wants to see you."

Buddha straightened up, a shrewd gleam spooling the possible reasons why around in his mind.

"What's he want, Smitty?"

"Ooh, tell ya the truth, I don't rightly know."

Ranklin winked off side at Buddha, turned to the guard, working sour against Buddha's sweet.

"What the fuck you mean, you don't know! You the motherfuckin' po-lice here, ain't you?"

"Awright now, Rank! You'd best mind your own business, when I got somethin' to say to you, I'll call your name 'n number, okay?"

Ranklin C. Jones, having spent a night dreaming of freedom and fast ladies, started to bristle up at the guard. Buddha, cooled him out.

"Rank, it's cool, baby. Warden probably needs my help to figure something out. I'll be ready in a minute, Smitty."

He changed into his pressed prison denims, brushed his teeth, and shot a natural comb through his receding hair line a few times.

"Okay, let's be gittin' on."

Smitty signalled to the control tower and manually unlocked Buddha's cell door. "Better watch your step, Rank," he grumbled through his slipping upper bridge.

"Shhhh-it! If you know what's good for you, you better watch your own fuckin' step. This is our prison, not yours."

Buddha and the guard fell into step, on the way to the warden's office, Buddha mentally reviewing his sins of the past week.

Wonder what the fuck he wants to see me about? That cocaine deal? Nawww, he wouldn't have any way of knowing about that. The prostitution set up? Nawww, it wouldn't be about that, what the hell do they care about punks setting up a union? The moonshine still in the kitchen? Naw, not that either, that's been there for years. What?

He maintained a poker face through all the check points, began to feel slightly nervous as they stood in front of the huge paneled door of the warden's office.

Smitty knocked politely, twice.

"Come in!" a big bass voice boomed.

"The Great—uhh, Chester Simmons, sir," Smitty announced, ushering him in.

"Come in! Come in, Buddha! Uhh, thank you, Smitherson, that'll be all."

The guard reluctantly departed, certain that this man be guarded everyday, that this passive storyteller was going to harm his warden in some way.

Buddha stood in the center of the floor, holding his cap behind his back, taking the warden's psychological measure. Big, bluff, bleary eyed beer drinker, three months in the Chair, tough as nails.

"Sit down, Buddha! Sit down! I know you're wonderin' why I wanted to see you. Coffee?"

"Yes, thank you, sir."

The warden bounced over to his intercom. "Pasquale, two expresso, please."

The Great Lawd Buddha relaxed, placed his cap on his left knee. Expresso, shit! Things couldn't be too bad, not if he was going to be treated to I-talian coffee before hand.

The telephone buzzed twice before the warden snatched it up. Trouble with a couple members of the population.

"Sock both of the bastards in the hole!" The warden growled, looking at Buddha as though he were a fellow warden, someone who understood the problems of managing the Big House.

Pasquale, the warden's personal servant, knocked lightly and popped in, balancing a tray of coffee cups and a pot of coffee, like the good Italo-European waiter he had been once upon a time.

"Pasquale, I don't wanna be disturbed for the next half hour," the warden warned as he pulled his swiveling armchair around to the front of his desk to sip with Buddha.

He handed him a demitasse, his ham hand folding over the tiny receptacle, poured one for himself and settled his beefy frame into his seat opposite Chester L. Simmons.

"Now then," he growled jovially, "lemme hear this story about you ruling the city of Tel Aviv for a week without anybody knowing about it. Anybody who can put anything over on them goddamn Jew bastards has got to have a helluva lot on the ball! Hahhh hahhh hahhh hahhh..."

The Great Lawd Buddha settled back in his seat, extremely distressed about the role he was being forced into, balanced his coffee cup on his thigh, an enigmatic smile on his face.

Uhhh huh, so this is what this mad motherfucker wants, a Scherharazade session, huh? Oh well, expresso is a helluva lot tastier than chickory dishwater in the mess hall. Guess I better tear that shit up I wrote last night, no one would believe it anyway.

He suavely held his cup out for a refill, pinky finger extended.

"Well, warden, you see, it was like this. I had copped a ride on this ol' broken down freighter, deliverin' coffee from Brazil to Haifa and...

Chapter 3

Chester L. Simmons, the Great Law Buddha, stood in line to board the bus going to Chicago, trying to remember the warden's last words. A hip ex-con had titled it "The Great Grey Speech," the speech delivered to departing members of 'the population'. Chester, after 15 years of incessant legal activity on his behalf by the eminent jailhouse lawyer, Victor Huge Feldman, was being released.

"Buddha, I just gotta say this, I've been a warden in somebody's prison for the last twenty two years and I've just gotta tell ya, I've never made the acquaintance of a finer prisoner than yourself."

Chester had stifled a belly laugh. A personal touch to the Great Grey Speech. They had had "pruno" cocktail parties on all three tiers, in addition to a bottle of good scotch, smuggled in under the benevolent eyes of the Great Grey Speechmaker. Fifteen years, from age 35 to 50, and now, thanks to the skillful manipulations of jailhouse lawyer

Numbah One, Victor Hugo Feldman, he was free. He made a mental note to write about the agony of the seven days prior to being released. It was exquisite agony, it was miserable—it was literally the "time" of my life—and I would never want to go through it again, not for all the tea in China.

Victor Hugo had discovered so many technicalities and discrepancies in the arrest, trial and conviction records, that he felt it was almost a miracle that they had been allowed to keep Chester incarcerated at all. They had even flirted with the idea of a suit.

"Victor, fuck a suit, just get me out of here."

And now he was free, riding on a ribbon of road that sliced through thousands of acres of springtime corn sprouts. He felt like a starving man looking at a gigantic table of food.

From time to time, he squeezed his eyes shut, to burn the sunlit images into his mind, to take the picture of what was passing by. The scene was almost too rich for his eyes.

He flashed back to his friends in the joint, the schools of people he had taught, the mean dudes who had challenged him, the brothers who had defended him, the hundreds of nights he had dreamed about walking down a street. Or circling a woman's waist with both arms.

He reopened his eyes to stare at the field, his mind nursing the hurt memory of Josie. Dear Josie, I don't know why I loved you so much more than the rest of them, but I did. It hurts me to think of you, to think that I am the one who ended your life, but I came to grips with that years ago and I no longer feel guilty about it. I feel a strange sense of detachment. I did what I did and that's that.

The hypnotic rumble of the bus flushed his mind in and out of past scenes, other emotions, different times. Sometimes he was a boy in Miss'ssippi, hanging a willow branch fishing pole into his favorite fishing hole. At other times he was the King of a Kingdom that his emotions had created, an exotic place set up for his fantasies. And finally, he was brutally pushed from his dreams by the driver making a blurred announcement that they were making a fifteen minute rest stop, in the middle of nowhere.

He exited the bus, feeling the bus equivalent of jet lag. He felt that he had come from a point so distant that it would've been impossible to reorient himself, even if he had the desire to do it. He was Out There, and nothing could take him back. It was alive, all of it, the thump-thump of the music coming from somewhere, the extremely colorful blouse of the woman walking in front of him, the bizarre language, behavior and dress of the people all around him. They gave him the impression of people in a circus, clowns. He wandered through the rest stop arcade, ignoring the rest stop food, the hamburgers, fries, cokes, come ons. He paused at the newsstand, the magazine sections, the pocketbook racks, felt stunned by the lasciviousness of the scene.

1974 to 1988. He felt like a dead man who'd been revived. Fifteen years popped up in front of him. They hadn't been dead years; he had kept abreast, as well as he could, but that was never quite what being "in it" was like. He was "in it" now and feeling slightly awkward.

After years of paying off in cigarettes, the cashier was saying, "that'll be $3.50, please." And he was slow about counting the money into her outstretched palm. It all seemed so meaningless.

He reclaimed his seat, feeling antagonistic, slightly out of sync. It was Now and Now was wrong; he could feel it. It wasn't Ancient Miss'ssippi racism, it was something else; this was class caste-money, against class non-recognition of caste and money.

He had felt the distinctions happen in prison, over a period of time, paying close attention to the inflow of prisoners. The latter day types, convicted of being caught, differed

59

monkedly from the "old timers," who had a commitment to "The System" and gave the impression (almost) that they were innocent until proven guilty. The latter day types all declared their guilt, with no moral hangovers, nothing to face down, but felt that they were being victimized, in light of what record "laboratory" discoveries had made about sin, corruption, guilt, money, Capitalism, bullshit and hype.

He read the sensational supermarket-bookstand-latest-this-is-the-latest novel in 45 minutes. It dripped from his hands.

The blurb stated that this was the bestseller of the supermarket bestsellers, and there was nothing lunny about Super-anything, cause that's what America reached for. Damn! No wonder shit is as fucked up as it is. He was beginning to feel "tuned in." Or rather "tuned back in," and he felt a profound distaste for what he was being exposed to.

He took the opportunity to urinate at the next stop and tried to ignore the blatantly racist headlines of the daily newspaper, "Palestinians Scurry for Cover as Israelis March Through."

"Chicago! Chicago! All off for Chicago! All others going on to..."

He made a deliberate effort to step off of the bus as though he were a "New Person." He had put the "New Person" together over the miles. The "New Person" wasn't going to be a "New Man," the guy that all of the theorists and new social designers were interested in already had something to work from, the "New Person" had been born with a fuckin' social defect, superior Poverty, and stepped out from there.

He knew it was going to be a "New Thang" and decided not to worry about it. Everything was Everythang, as the eminently blessed "New Person," Donny Hathaway had put it. Yes, Everythang was Everythang...

The bus station delighted him, the succession of would-be-do-it-to-your salesmen, serious brothers, junkies to the extreme, drug addicts. He was suddenly immersed in something that he could understand. Strange, he thought, how transparent dope fiends are; they could approach you about anything in the world, and if you could get into where they were comin' from, drug addiction meant nothing.

He had taken one of the drug panhandlers off to one side, a deeply addicted black Black man who looked like a Masai warrior, and talked deep shit to him. He felt he had no choice, behind the fact that the brother was trying to rip him off.

"Awright, hold on now, brotherman, you didn't get my shit! Okay? Now what I want you to look at, if I was 'the usual people,' your ass would be doin' the normal six month wrap for whatever." He felt real pissed to discover that his stuff had been ripped off while he had been making his dedicated give up dope speech. Moments after the realization, he went from feeling a need for outrageous revenge, to the upper case thought of Freedom.

Freedom meant finding a place to live, shopping for groceries, "making ends meet," coping. He strolled out of the bus station, minus his two pieces of luggage, into downtown Chicago. Glad I kept my notebook in hand.

"Wowwww!" he involuntarily exclaimed, exiting the bus station. The sight of the people rushing past, in all the directions at the same time, almost filled him with panic. He had forgotten how frenzied life could be, how crazed the activities of people were.

He wandered over to Michigan Avenue, feeling free, his movement unrestricted by walls, guards, other prisoners. What to do? On Michigan Avenue, he strolled South, drawn to the Art Institute's announced display of Impressionists. He paid the entrance fee and strolled in, his senses tuned to a peak. Two hours later he strolled out, overwhelmed by the colors. He stood on the steps of the Art Institute, dazed,

61

trying to reorient himself.

What better way to start the first day of being on the streets?

He patted his money belt and pulled out the address of the halfway house he had been given. Time to go home.

"How do you do, Chester, my name is just what it says right here on my name plate, Steve Bell. We were given notice that you'd be coming our way and so, hahh hahh hahh, we fixed a suite up for you."

A big white jerk, that was the immediate conclusion he reached, listening to the man sitting across from him.

"The rules are few and simple, like my old sergeant used to say, 'keep it simple stupid.' Hahhh hahh, wise guy, that sergeant."

"Sounds almost like an old guard I used to have, who used to say, 'don't speak until I tell you.' "

"Don't speak until...hahhh hahh, I like that, hahhh hahhh hah. Now then, you're entitled to a four month stay here and believe me, with the kind of low rates we charge this place is a real savings heaven. We figure that a fella should be on his feet after four months and if he isn't, for some reason, we have a committee review his case and if he warrants it, we can give him another quarter."

Chester felt drowsy, lulled into a semi-hibernatory state by the big white jerk's rambling talk.

"We don't allow women in the rooms past 10:00 p.m., no smoking of left handed cigarettes, hahhh hahh, 'left handed cigarettes,' get it?"

"Only right handed cigarettes."

"Only right handed cigarettes, hahh hahh. I like that. Now then, getting back to the rules, drinking. We know a fella wants to have a beer from time to time, but we don't want parties, if you know what I mean?"

"I do know what you mean."

"If you find that you have to be out overnight for some reason, we should be notified before ten o'clock."

"Why?"

The big white jerk pursed his lips, shuffled his shoulders uncomfortably.

"Why? Well, those are the rules."

"But why is there a rule that says you have to be notified if I'm going to be out overnight, before ten?"

Once again the lips pursed, the shoulders shuffled.

"Hmmmmmm, that's a tuffie, hahh hahh. Never been asked that one before, maybe it's because..." The big white man wiped imaginary beads of sweat from his brow. "Wowww! You had me by the short hairs there for a minute."

Chester smiled, this was going to be easy.

A half hour later, after the Bowman House rules had been laboriously spelled out, he was escorted to a room on the second floor. Bowman House, on the western fringe of Hyde Park, had once been a fifteen room mansion. It was now a halfway house with twenty five rooms.

"We don't have a dining room, as such, but I usually keep a pot of coffee on in the kitchen and the guys keep a fund going on for rolls, donuts, stuff like that. I notice you don't have any bags with you."

"I got ripped off at the bus station."

The big man shook his head sadly.

"Wouldn't this be a better world if people didn't steal? Well, in any case, welcome to Bowman House." They shook hands in front of his room door and Steve lumbered off to do something else.

Chester opened the door of his room, deposited his notebook on the bed, closed the door, opened it again and finally closed it. He felt exhilirated to be able to close a door after all the years someone else had opened and closed his cell door. A bed, a bedside lamp, desk and chair in front of the only window in the room, a closet. A place to sleep and scribble. He pulled his shoes off and sprawled out on the bed, stood to look out the window. Great midwestern trees, a quiet street, a few people strolling past. He sprawled back on the bed, his heart pumping as though he had just run up and down ten flights of stairs.

I'm free! Good God Almighty, I'm free!

He made a careful study of himself in the mirror. I oughta be able to pull something, somebody, from somewhere.

He was in his second week of being on the outside and aside from meeting the assorted bag of men who were living in Bowman House and making job applications...

"You say you've been a seaman for the past fifteen years?"

"Yes, I was sailing the seven seas on the good ship Lollipop."

It was not going to be quite as easy as he thought it would be, but there was still hope, and the security guard deal (in the Bank parking lot) looked like a sure thing. It would have to do until the real thing came along. Meanwhile, it was Friday night and he was feeling the urge. Think I'll trip over to this bohemian joint everybody's been tellin' me about.

"Taking in a little night air, huh, Chester?"

"Yeah, Steve, gonna get out here and sniff the breezes for a bit. I'll let you know if I wind up staying out overnight, okay?"

"Uhh, yeah, Chester, whatever you say."

It had only take a few days to convert big Steve Bell. He was like a little boy who needed lots of attention.

Chester strolled deeper into Hyde Park, just another male Black citizen with slanted eyes and a bit of paunch, about 5'10", an ex-con. He was beginning to feel the rhythms of the city much better, the bedlam decibel noise level, the casual lack of respect that people showed for each other. He had made the analogy between the 'inside' and the 'outside' several times. If someone in the joint had behaved, misbehaved toward a fellow inmate, in the way that people habitually behaved on the outside, the yard would've been littered with the dead and the dying. He couldn't seem to remember if this behavior, the impoliteness, the brusqueness, the pushing and shoving, was in evidence before he was removed from the scene.

No, he concluded, it hadn't been like this. People had been, to use a cliche, more civilized. There were always arrogant, spiteful, nasty people, but never an entire population. The tensions, drive-by shootings, the prevalence of weird drugs, violent gangs, the casualness of the violence disturbed him.

"Lovely evenin,' isn't it?"

The gentleness of the remark jarred him. A middle-aged white woman walking one of those small shaggy dogs they seemed to be addicted to.

"Yes, it is a lovely evening," he replied, feeling the truth of it.

It *was* a lovely evening. The hint of a breeze from the lake, a balmy evening.

Jakes. He walked in, crumbling cast off peanut shells underfoot, headed for the bar.

So, this is the bohemian joint.

"What'll it be, mister?"

"Uhh, a gin 'n tonic."

He studied the layout: a roomy joint, chess players on the north wall, hairy university types with quart pitchers of beer on their table, some kind of syrupy classical music oozing out of the system, several racially mixed couples, frenzied conversations. A young Black man sitting with a gorgeously shaped Asian girl caught his eye. She didn't get a body like that eating rice and tofu.

7:30 p.m.

He looked into the mirror behind the bar, studying the faces of the two people who'd popped up onto the two stools to his right. One was Black, the other white and they were both women, but there was something hard and mannish about their mannerisms.

Bulldaggers? Hard to say. That was something else he had noticed about the scene. Women didn't seem to be what they had once been, none of them, Black, white, or any other color. They seemed to be almost too assertive, aggressive, manly. He turned to them, after his third gin and tonic.

"Lovely evening, isn't it?"

They paused in the middle of sipping their beers. The one nearest to him spoke. "I suppose one could say that, if we ignored the latest reports of world hunger, the current warfare going on in eight places, the dreary state of the economy, police oppression, scandals in the government, innocent people dying from lack of clean drinking water and about ten other things I won't bother to belabor your head with."

He had struck gold, somebody to rap with.

"You're absolutely right, I guess I was just comin' from a state of mind, rather than giving any concern for what mind the state was in."

A half hour and two more gin and tonics later, they had become Buddha, Sharlie and Edwina "call me Ed."

And they weren't lesbians. He had picked that up from the drift of the conversation.

"A man has to have that certain kind of quality about him, you know what I mean? I mean, it's something I think a dude is born with."

Sharlie was a freelance photographer and Ed was a bus driver.

"What do you do, Buddha? I love that, 'Buddha'."

"Hahhh hah, well, at the moment I'm ungainfully unemployed."

"Well, what did you do when you were employed?"

He fixed his eyes on his face in the mirror for a minute.

"This may sound strange to you," he spoke solemnly, "but I've never had a job."

Sharlie the freelance photographers tossed a few peanut shells on the floor contemptuously. "Fuck a job! Jobs are just to make utilities money. What did you do?"

"I was a complete liar," he announced.

They were strangers, they were nice people, lovely ladies, once you got past the butch hairdos and the rough coating. Both of them cracked up.

"You're serious!"

"Yes, I am. I lied my way from one end of the country to the other."

"Wowww! I like that better than driving a bus."

"It doesn't pay as well, believe me."

"What the hell does pay mean, if your time belongs to somebody else?"

Ed, noticing that her drink was down, ordered another round. "Buddha, you talk like my kinda guy!" She reached across and slapped him jovially between the shoulder blades. The pain made him dizzy for a couple beats. A few more drinks later, their heads had formed a tight triangle, sharing a whispered suggestion by Sharlie.

"Look, all this boozin' is okay, if that's what you dig, but I've got something much better."

Ed clapped her hands gleefully. "Oh great! You did get it?"

"This morning in the mail."

In the mail? Chester plastered his opaque look on.

"Ahhem, Buddha, do you get high? I know you do."

67

He went deadpan on the question. "I've been known to have a glass of sherry, from time to time."

"This guy's too much. C'mon, let's get outta here. Where've you parked?"

"I ain't."

"Good, you can ride with us, I live about eight blocks from here."

He slid off the bar stool, feeling giddy, pleasantly lit, and pulled out a slender roll of bills to pay for his tab.

Ed called to the bartender, "Put this on the tab, Mac!"

He strolled out of Jakes behind the two, feeling so macho he wanted to drum on his chest. They were tallish, wore form fitting pants, had beautiful asses and acted like sailors on leave. He was pleased with the mix.

The stuff that Sharlie had received in the mail came straight from Bangkok, two sticks of extremely potent marijuana stuffed into the pages of a magazine and sealed with wax paper. He strolled around the apartment while the two women sniffed, ooohed, ahhhed and rolled up the herb. Beautiful apartment, varnished hardwood floors, Afro-Danish designed furniture, tasteful.

"Sharlie, this your work on the wall here?"

"Yeah, some of it. There's a portfolio of stuff over there on the table, by the window."

He turned the pages, stunned by the sensitivity of the work. She had female nudes, beautifully lit and posed, old people, babies with very wise expressions, nature shots, dancers.

Ed and Sharlie joined him at the table, a joint for each. It smelled like a rare kind of tobacco. They lit him up.

"Phewwww! You are a helluva photographer and this is some of the baddest smoke I've ever had!"

They shared conspiratorial grins, a little giddy already.

"How the hell do you get that dope?"

Sharlie went over to the Danish coffee table, picked up

the magazine, the wax wrap, the padded envelope cover. "It comes in this, simple as that."

"I mean, but..."

"Buddha, they can't check every package that comes through the U.S. mails, if they did the post office would spill over. A friend of mine whose trippin' around in Southeast Asia can mail me a lil' stick or some Laotian red from time to time. He puts a fake return address on it and if they should ever bird dog it to me all I'd have to do is say I don't know what the fuck it's all about, some shit delivered to me by mistake."

Ed wandered over to the stereo sound system, pulled out a tape and turned it on. Chester sank down onto the sofa, tears sprang to his eyes as Charlie Parker's "Lover" spilled out at him. The two women exchanged looks and settled into seats near him, Ed sat beside him on the sofa.

"That's Bird. He kinda gets to me when I haven't heard him for a while."

They took simultaneous hits and sat silently for a few minutes, feasting on the sounds.

"Buddha, you act like a man who enjoys life, you know?"

He framed a wry smile. "Baby, when you've been away from life as long as I have, everything is doubly enjoyable."

"Where've you been?" Ed probed quietly.

"I been in jail for the last fifteen years."

The words seemed to melt into the music, the music into the words. The two women stared at his downcast eyes. He had made a conscious decision to stop lying, if it were not going to be harmful to his best interests.

"Fifteen years is a long ass time," Sharlie said, firing up the last fourth of the joint.

"Yes, it sho' is," he agreed.

"I know this may seem impertinent but..."

"What did I do? I committed a crime of passion. I shot

69

the woman I was in love with."

. The two women seemed to breathe a collective sigh of relief.

"I guess that's something that could happen to anybody."

"If Kenneth had stuck around here another week I'm sure I would've offed his ass!"

The two women shared an injoke, Chester caught the tail end and joined them. What the hell was there to be maudlin about? He was free.

"How long you been out?" Sharlie asked suddenly.

"Well, lemme see now, if I counted today, it would be exactly two weeks."

"You...you just got out!"

"Yep, like it was yesterday."

Once again, sympathetic expressions covered their faces. Sharlie broke the moment with an announcement.

"Hey, I don't know about you guys but I'm feelin' a little snackish. Anybody else got the munchies?"

"I'm with you, girlfriend."

"Buddha, pick whatever you wanna hear out of the case there."

Bird ended with "April in Paris," as they quickly moved into the kitchen and closed the door. He stood up and felt his head go through the ceiling for a second.

Wowww, talk about good dope! Wait til I tell Brian, Donnell and Marcus about this. The thought of his friends glued him in place. I can't tell them about this, they would think I was lying.

"Buddha," Sharlie called through the partially opened door.

"Yeah?"

"Buddha, Ed wants to know if you had any homosexual encounters, uhh, experiences, while you were in jail?"

Chester chuckled, pulling tapes out. Damn! I need my

70

specs. "Yeahhh, I had one constant love affair with a guy named Mr. Goodhand."

He could hear them cracking up in the kitchen. Damn! I really lucked up on two live wires this evening. He placed John Coltran's "Africa Brass" on the deck and resumed his place on the sofa.

'Trane!! Trane! Trane! 'Trane!

"Buddha!"

"Yeahhh!" This was beginning to be kinda fun.

"Sharlie wants to know if you've had sex with a woman since you've been out?"

It was his turn to laugh. "Hahh hah hah. No! Believe it or not, I've been too busy trying to find a job to try to find a woman."

'Trane! 'Trane! Trane! 'Trane! The intensity of the playing, the depth of the feelings, the emotional strength of him. 'Trane.

They swayed out of the kitchen, in time to the music, each of them carrying a tray, naked. They carefully placed the trays, loaded with small sandwiches, cheese slices and beer on the coffee table and resumed their places near him.

He decided to play the nutroll, and pretend that nothing unusual was happening.

"Why did you wanna know if I had had a homo thang?"

"Cause that might have meant that you were in a high risk group, disease-wise."

"Oh, I see. And how about this question about me being with a woman?"

Ed leaned over and began to unbutton his shirt. "Well, that would take a bit of an edge off things, don't you think?"

He stood, shook his pants down around his ankles and swiftly removed shoes, socks, jockey shorts. When he was naked too, he held his arms out to gather them in, tears streaming down his cheeks.

71

"You all are some righteously beautiful sisters, you know that?"

Sharlie pointed a high intensity lamp up at the ceiling and beckoned them to follow her to the bedroom.

He leaned against the low stone wall, circling the bank parking lot with his eyes, feeling slightly silly even after two weeks in his guard uniform. It was worse than doing time because there was nothing to do but stand there, stroll around, keeping an open eye for "suspicious characters."

They had prohibited him from writing on the job. "How are you going to keep an eye out for suspicious characters, Mr. Simmons, if you're trying to write the Great American Novel?"

Seven dollars and fifty cents an hour to stand around. He felt certain that the guard service ("Trustworthy, honest, alert") knew he would never attempt to prevent a bank robbery with a night stick. Or even with a pistol, if they had issued him one.

He strolled the perimeter of the parking lot, his arms folded across his chest. "Please don't keep your hands in your pockets, Mr. Simmons, it presents an image." He nodded pleasantly at the regulars. A real North American situation, poor people being underpaid to protect people with money. Or their property. He returned to his starting point, the idea for a short story buzzing around in his brain, feeling frustrated.

Wonder what Ed and Sharlie are up to? He plunged his hands into his pockets for a beat, suddenly remembered the rule and took them out. Beautiful, talented, crazy, outrageous women. It had taken him a week of leaving messages on Sharlie's machine before he had finally managed to catch the lady herself.

"When're we gonna get together for a return engagement?''

She had given him a circumnavigational trip which spelled out—hey, that was just a moment, don't even think about return engagements.

"Well, we can get together at Jakes then, huh?"

"Whenever. Look, I got a shoot to do. Talk to you."

Women. He doubted if they knew why they did whatever they did. Maybe ol' Patcheye is right, women are just victims of the moon, lunacy, lunatics.

"'Scuse me, Mr. Simmons. Mr. Simmons?" Greyson, the 2nd Vice President again.

"Yes, what is it, Mr. Greyson?"

"Ahh, have you checked the perimeters of the lot within the past half hour?"

"I have checked the perimeters of the lot twice within the past half hour, and four times in the half hour before that."

"There's no need to become testy about the question, Mr. Simmons."

"I am not becoming testy, Mr. Greyson, I am becoming very goddamned irritated at you coming out here to bug the fuck out of me every few minutes."

He watched the effect of his carefully chosen speech. Greyson's hairline seemed to recede, his thin lips went white and red splotches flashed on his face. He was livid with anger.

"Mr. Simmons, I'm going to speak with your superior about your conduct."

Chester took one menacing step toward the man, causing him to back away in fear and then walk as fast as he could back into the bank.

Little asshole. He took another stroll around the perimeter, his hands plunged into his pockets, a grim smile on his face.

Chapter 4

"Awwww what the hell! Chester, it was just a lil' ol' security guard job. You're a smart guy, you can do better than that."

"Hope you're right, Steve, hope you're right. Well, thanks for the tea 'n sympathy, chum. Time for me to call it a night, got a big day at the employment office tomorrow."

"Talk to ya later, Chester."

He sat at the desk in front of the open window, the lights off, enjoying the rustle of the tree leaves, the sounds of the outside, the sight of a window without bars.

He felt panicky, anxious for long moments.

What am I supposed to do? What am I qualified to do?

He quieted the panic down and folded his hands on the desk for an objective review of his background, of what he had skills for.

Mississippi, going to the one room school house, fleeing the lynch mob. Nothing skilled about that, just a survival tactic. The north, odd jobs, a salesman, money to be made if you were willing to lie, lie, lie. I'm sick of lying.

Five years with Josie, she supported us, reluctantly, while I pretended to write; writing was my game. He had made two efforts to do his autobiography, which would've been brimful of lies; one Josie had thrown away and the second one he had destroyed. Once again, just as he had admitted to Sharlie and Ed, he was a born liar and that,s all. His jawline hardened, looking up at the mocking half moon.

One damn thing is certain, I'm not going to sell my time for a few bucks a day, I've already done that. The big white jerk, (sorry 'bout that, Steve), is right, I'm too smart for that penny ante crap.

He began to undress, a few schemes swirling around in his head for the first time since he had been released.

"The fire you return to is always ashes, the fire . . ." The proverb stuck in his head as he walked east on Fourth Street, from King Drive to Drexel Boulevard.

Everything had changed for the worse. The area seemed to be in the violent grip of some kind of architectural upheaval, some going up, others going down. He assumed that the usual inner city number was being pulled off. The whites, having rediscovered how much closer the slums were to their jobs, were reclaiming the slums by declaring them unfit for human habitation and then declaring them habitable after they had rebuilt.

Clever game.

He checked the man's eyes out as he strolled past him. He was up to no good. He plunged his hands into his windbreaker to grip his knife.

Ten yards past, the man still stood in the doorway, and then he called out.

"The Great Lawd Buddha!"

Chester released his grip on his knife, it had to be somebody from the old days, no one could possibly call him that but one of the old timers.

"Are you addressing me, my friend?"

The man rushed toward him, a smile full of broken teeth, a tattered look about him.

"It's me, Buddha, Chico Daddy, you know, from the Afro-Lords?"

Chester stared at the young-old man shuffling up to him. Chico Daddy, one of the young dudes I used to do my Sherharazade number for.

"Well, I'll be damned! Chico Daddy! What's happening?!"

They shook hands, cautiously taking each other's measure.

"Buddha, yeahhh. I said to myself when you walk past, 'Damn! That look like the Great Lawd Buddha.'"

Chester took in the wasted form, the shifting eyes. Heroin. Or crack. Or maybe both.

"When you get out, man?"

"'Bout a month ago."

"You know I was out there, with the rest of the Lords, the night...you know, the night the scene went down."

"Yeahhh, I remember you being there. Where is the rest of the gang? I used to get a kite from Billy every now 'n then."

"Awwww man, them dudes went with the wind. Sherman got off into track, went to some funny named college in Tennessee, won a lot o' medals 'n shit. Last I heard he was still down there, married 'n shit. Burkes is still on the set, I see him every now 'n then. BoBo got off heavy into that wine 'n shit, and last I heard Billy was living way out south somewhere."

"How old are you now, Chico?"

"I'm thirty now."

77

"Thirty?"

"Yeahhh, thirty moons. Hah hah."

Chester watched the "dope fiend fidget" develop, the urge for that next fix creeping up his back.

"Where you on your way, Buddha?"

"Just taking a walk down memory lane, that's all."

"Yeahhh, I heard that. But look, man, I wouldn't be walkin' around here too much, they got a different bunch o' dudes 'n shit, and they'll rip anybody off."

"Yeahhh, I heard that. Well, Chico, it was good seeing you, take care."

"Awright, later on, Buddha."

He watched Chico Daddy break into the "junky jog," a kind of coolie shuffle with a dip in the middle, a motion that they could maintain for blocks.

Heroin, cocaine, wine, whiskey, beer, pills, dreams—something for everybody.

He got back on the bus at Drexel Boulevard, the money scheme swirling around in his head even harder. The realization struck him halfway to his destination. I can't stay here, this shit is dead and stinkin'! I got to get out of here. He suddenly felt exhilirated by the idea of leaving Chicago, of leaving the state. Maybe I'll leave the country. The thought sobered him.

Maybe I'll leave the country. But where can I go with four hundred dollars? He found himself smiling, looking out at the once grand homes on Drexel Boulevard. How many times have I lied about going somewhere without a dime?

He strode into Bowman House feeling like a man with a purpose.

"Hey, Chester, how'd it go?"

"I'll tell you about it later."

He raced into his room, pulled out a dog eared Atlas and stared at the United States, Canada and Mexico.

78

Canada gets cold, no cold for the kid. Mexico? His eyes wandered into the Carribbean basin and back to Mexico. Don't have to have a boat to get there.

He traced a line with his finger, from Illinois to California.

That's what I'll do, I'll get down into it from California.

He sat on the side of the bed and slowly lowered his back to the mattress, feeling as though he had already accomplished something grand.

First thing I have to do is work out a way to get out there without spending any money. I'll talk to Steve, he seems to have a lot of odd information.

It was falling into place. He laced his hands behind his head and stared out the window.

Yeahhh, its falling into place, for the first time in fifteen years.

"You might check this auto driving thing out. Or you might go over to the University and check the bulletin board, those kids are always traipsin' off to Florida or California, somewhere."

"Steve, you know something?"

"Naw, what?"

"You *know* something!"

Steve made an uncharacteristically hip soul spank on Chester's outstretched hand. The man was full of surprises. But what the hell could you expect from a guy who had been dealing with recently freed ex-convicts for the past ten years?

He made up an immediate list of things to do: A) driver's license, B) apply for as many I.D.'s as possible. "White folks," said Rank B. Jones, ex-con man, "love to see I.D., any kind."

He struck gold exactly seven days later, on the bulletin board of the International Student Center.

"Three riders needed, to share expenses for trip to Taos,

79

New Mexico. Contact Johnny Lambert III or Bert Candles at 761-1792."

"Yes, this is Bert Candles, Johnny isn't in at the moment. Oh, the New Mexico trip? Okay, you're number three on the list. We're gonna be havin' a meeting this Sunday morning, about elevenish, sort of a get acquainted session. That okay with you?"

"Sure, that'll be fine, Bert."

"Swell, the address is 5327 University Avenue, apartment 207."

"Great, see you then, Bert."

He left the telephone booth feeling full of life, adventurous. It was possible to make anything happen, if you had enough faith and energy. Sunday, two days from now. Well, I can give up this job hunting charade and start planning my escape from the Land of Snows. Taos, New Mexico, just a dog trot from Los Angeles. He wandered over onto the lakefront, in the wake of screaming children and thousands of sun worshippers. Damn, looks like a lot of folks took off from work today. He strolled along the beach front promenade, alternately trying to put a thrive-in-California game together and pausing to stare at one spectacularly shaped body after another.

Every fine sister in the city must be out here today. Wonder what Sharlie and Ed are doing tonight?

He briefly flirted with the idea of calling Sharlie. Nawww. It wouldn't make any sense, they already gave me whatever they were gonna give me, a couple wild and crazy ladies, without a doubt.

He sat on a bench and stared out over the Lake.

Here I am now, a fifty year old ex-convict, no real trade, skill, or occupation. He dismissed his editorship of the prison newspaper for five years as a miscarriage of justice.

"Warden wants you to run the paper, Buddha."

"Why mè, Smitty?"

"Well, I guess cause Longfellow got it in the back yesterday."

"I know about that, but why me for the paper?"

"I guess it's cause he likes you, Buddha."

The only thing I really know how to do is tell stories. He was never certain that he could write them as well as he could tell them because he had never gotten too deeply into the craft of writing, and he had too much respect for the art to fake it. If that could be done.

The prison newspaper had been a piece of cake, each position (except his) filled by a qualified member of the journalistic profession. He had been a true figurehead.

August, hot and humid. He looked right and left at the people on the promenade.

Enjoy it now, folks, cause two months from now you gonna feel like you're in Siberia. He smiled, unkinking his body from the bench.

Damn, I'm gonna have to start doing some exercises, get my psychique in shape for the American Riviera.

He put on his brightest face for the person answering the door.

"Yes?"

"The name is Chester L. Simmons."

"Oh! Ohh! Yes, please come in."

His eyes, cameras for the scene, took in the freeze frame action of the four upper middle (maybe rich) twenty year olds as they swiveled their necks around to look at him. He decided to take charge, overwhelm their surprise.

"Hi, everybody! My name is Chester L. Simmons, my friends call me Buddha."

Good. They weren't conscious racists, just clean cut young white kids who thought that middle aged Black men only existed on TV or in their dad's work force.

"Uhh, I'm Johnny Lambert the third, lemme introduce you to the rest of the guys."

They were drinking a little jug wine, eating cheese and funny crackers, no evidence of dope. Good.

"Bert Candles, my roomie."

"Hi ya doin', Bert, we spoke on the phone."

"Right, how's it goin'?"

"Suzy Franks, our resident feminist."

"Gimme a break, pleeezz! Hi, how are you?"

"And this is Marvin Swanson, he's into pre-med, which means that we'll have someone to nurse our cuts and prescribe stuff to keep us awake. Have a seat, have a glass of wine. We were just kinda gettin' into who we are, that kinda thing. We know each other from school but we've never made a cross-country trip together."

He slid into a convenient niche on the sofa, no sense trying to do that Yogi-Lotus they were doing. Somebody passed him a goblet of wine. He glanced around at the furnishings. Almost a duplicate of Sharlie's, must be a Hyde Park trend. A well stocked bookcase, lots of film books.

"Suzy, we were about to listen to your reason for wanting to make this trip?"

"Well, aside from the fact that when I heard that you and Bert were gonna go to Taos, the top chauvinists on campus, I..." She paused for their sarcastic laughter, obviously a banter they shared often. "Seriously, as a budding architect, no pun intended, I felt I had to make this trip because the architecture of the Southwest, going back to the Pueblo Indian apartments, is some of the most imaginative in the whole country. I couldn't miss it."

"Marv?"

"Yeah, well, as you all know, this is gonna be the last time for a few years that I'll have a chance to hang out, drink a little beer, after that it's more urology than I'm ever gonna need for a lifetime. That's why I'm up for the trip, to climb a few hills, drink a little beer.''

They turned to Chester with differing degrees of interest, Johnny looked slightly scared. He felt a lie swell up in his mouth, I'm a psychologist on sabbatical who wants to study young whites driving to Taos, and swallowed it.

"Well, my turn, huh? I guess, to be really honest with you, I don't really know exactly why I'm going to Taos, except that it'll put me within hollerin' distance of L.A. and I couldn't figure a more interesting way to go than with other people.''

Marvin, the pre-med beer drinker, applauded.

"I like that, I like that.''

Johnny's hesitancy seemed to resolve itself.

"Okay, we all know why we're going. Or we don't. I didn't mention it, Chester...''

"You can call me Buddha.''

"You weren't here when Bert and I explained that we wanted to make like a documentary of our trip. Kind of a picaresque home film, in a sense. We'll have some set situations we'll be wantin' to have you guys get into but mainly we just want to be creative.''

"Too bad they don't dish grants out to architects the way they do to filmmakers," Suzy stated with fake hostility.

"Eat your heart out, Suzy Franks. Okay, guys,'' Johnny the Director raised his voice, "I think we got five congenial souls, if anybody has any objection to anybody being included, let's spit it out now or forever hold your spit.''

Chester smiled up at the tall, slender, blonde, blue-eyed filmmaker. Hmmmmm, I like this kid.

The looked around at each other and smiled. Bert Candles slipped him a seductive wink. Hmmmmm.

"Okay, no objections, good. Now then, let's go on to step

two. Bert is gonna collect a hundred bucks from each of you. This will cover everything. We got a VW van, which means we're gonna be doin' a lot of upright sleeping. We're also gonna be doing a lot of rest top catnappin' and picknicking. We've figured it out so that if we rotate the driving properly, we'll be in pretty good shape when we arrive. We'd advise you to take a few warm sweaters, a jacket or two maybe, the nights can be chilly. One final word, any expense that's incurred beyond the fare we're charging will be covered by Bert and myself, fair enough?''

Suzy, Marvin and Chester spontaneously raised their wine glasses in a toast.

''Oh, one final final word, do all your smokin' and boozin' before we leave because afterwards we're just gonna limit ourselves to an occasional roadside beer. The police are looking for four young white kids and a middle aged Black dude who looks like a Japanese guy.''

They all enjoyed the crack, Chester most of all. These were the New Whites, very different from the Old Whites.

''When are we leaving?''

''Middle of the week, Wednesday night, less traffic than the weekend. We should be there by next Sunday.''

Damn, these kids were on the move. Well, that's fine with me, the sooner the better.

Chester walked through Hyde Park, overtaken by a slight trip hammering heart. What if it were all a scam? What if he showed up Wednesday night and they weren't there? What if they had simply beat him out of a hundred bucks?

He was tempted to turn around and check on the situation. Nahhh, these are po' little rich kids, they'd be scammin' for major league bucks if anything. Nothing to do but shape up to move out.

Steve had advised him to buy a surplus Army duffel bag and shown him how to pack it.

"Only thing you can't pack in here, Buddha, is a good piece of pussy."

"Gimme time, Steve, I'll figure out a way."

He thought he detected a real sense of sympathy as he shook hands with the three men he had developed a "Hi and Bye" relationship during his short stay at Bowman House.

"I'll give you a lift over there, Buddha, might be kinda hard luggin' that duffel bag that far."

"Thanks, Steve, appreciate it."

They drove through the Hyde Park area, making small talk, Chester feeling more anxious by the minute. What if it were a scam?

Not to worry. They were waiting for him.

"Hi, Buddha. Just in time, man, everybody's here."

"Well, Steverino, this looks like where I get off and join another trolley."

"Buddha, it's been great knowin' you, guy. Come back through next time you're in town."

"Will do. Take it easy."

"Yeah, you too."

They were so well organized he felt that he was part of a military expedition. Water, non-perishable foods packed, extra sleeping bags (he hadn't even thought about that!), two five gallon cans of gas strapped to the rear, a typed list of the driving order. The rotation started off with Candles and ended with Simmons, which meant he'd be free to sightsee until late the following day.

"Mind if I sit next to you for the first few hundred miles?" asked Suzy.

"Not at all, there's plenty room."

He took a close look at Suzy Franks. Big boned Jewish girl, lush mouth, big shapely breasts (she'll look like a cow

He took a close look at Suzy Franks. Big boned Jewish

85

girl, lush mouth, big shapely breasts (she'll look like a cow in ten years), ass on her like a sister. And intelligent to boot. It looked like an interesting trip.

He could see something settling in place already. She and Johnny were "pals." Bert seemed to be a little "sweet" and Marvin was asleep already.

She smiled at him and made an eloquent shrug, as though to say, looks like me 'n you, babe.

"Seat belts all in place? Anybody gotta take a leak? Okay, here we go!"

They were on the road.

"Who are you, Buddha, and where did you come from, and what were you when you were there?" Suzy asked, paraphrasing Bogart in Casablanca.

Yes, this was going to be a nice little trip. He moved a few inches closer and started talking to her in his lowest, most hypnotic, story-rapper's voice.

"Suzy, let me take you back to what I'll call duh beginnin'..."

He released her two and a half hours later, her lower jaw dangling, her eyes glazed from his storytelling. He sighed and leaned his head back against the rest. He had only mixed two, three small lies into the recipe, little linch pins for transitional purposes. He had told the absolute truth for two and a half hours. He was emotionally drained from the effort.

He nodded off thinking about prison. Two a.m., what would I be doing at two a.m.? Probably looking up at the ceiling, awakened by some maniac screaming. Or simply thinking about what it would be like to be free again. He had often thought about Nelson Mandela in jail.

He and a number of other politically sophisticated inmates.

"Man, can you imagine what that brother must've went through? I mean, it's bad enough to be in the joint unjustly, but not to have any idea when you're gonna get out. What do you think kept him together?''

"His mind, no doubt about it. If he hadn't decided that he was gonna stay together he would've gone to pieces by the first year.''

He yawned himself awake at dawn, checked the white woman's head on his shoulder and felt disoriented for a beat.

Dawn coming over the corn fields of Illinois. Marvin, obviously a real sleep lover, yawned, stretched, and folded himself back into a fetal knot.

Johnny looked at him in the rearview mirror, flashed him a smile. They had changed drivers sometime during the night. So far, so good.

Suzy Franks stifled a yawn and smiled into his face. He smiled back. Once again he found himself thinking about how different the New Whites were from the Old Whites. And it didn't have a helluva lot to do with the age thing, it was more psycho-philosophical than anything else. It was as though they had dealt with the history of their race in America, wrestled with all of the demons and made a conscious decision to come out the other side. He felt good about them, pleased that he wasn't going to have to browbeat, verbally fist fight from Chicago to Taos, New Mexico.

"Buddha?''

"Yeah, Suzy.''

"You know I went to sleep last night, this morning . . . God! Look at that! An old fashioned barn!''

Marvin Swanson, the pre-med guy perked up, glanced out at the barn they were passing, frowned at the budding architect and curbed into another position.

"'Sorry 'bout that,'' she cast her eyes down demurely, the modern woman playing shy.

"You were saying, before the barn?''

"Uhh yeah, I was just going to say that you really laid a lot on my head last night, you know?''

"How so?" The dawn was breaking into a beautifully sunny day.

"Well, hey, let's face it, people like me, like us," she gestured round, "don't ordinarily meet dudes like you. I mean, shit, let's face it, the naughtiest thing I've done in twenty four years is to give a dude some leg without using a condom. And I think I must've had every kind of test in the world for about six months after that."

Chester stared into her saucer blue eyes for a minute, thinking. "Suzy, was that the only time you'd had sex without a rubber?"

"Well, other than when my Uncle Morrie molested me."

Marvin slowly came alive, speaking emphatically. "I have *never* had intercourse without protection."

"Me neither," Johnny chimed in from the driver's seat. Bert was asleep. Or was pretending to be asleep.

"Suzy, you're twenty four, Johnny you're?"

"Twenty four."

"And I'm twenty two. And Bert is twenty three."

"And all of you guys are sexually active."

"Some of us are more sexually active than others," Marvin answered, with a deliberately sly look at Suzy.

Bert stirred himself awake, took a look out at the passing scenery and started passing breakfast around, sandwiches and mineral water.

Chester felt expansive, it was a new day. He was free, traveling with fast minds and his brain was self-designing a way for him to make a hit out of California. "Would anyone in here be offended if I used profane language, obscene terms?" he asked jokingly.

They all answered him by bursting into a multi-faceted song, English Pub style.

Suzy: O fuchs! O gee good goddam let's fuck! O fucks!

Bert: O shucks! Motherfuckers fuck! O gee goddam let's

fuck! Doodoo Pee Pee shit! sonovabitch!

Johnny: Ass Ass Ass eatin' ass, how crass! How about some shit! shit! shit! shit!

Marvin: The skin of your dick is sore, you must've caught something from a dirty whore! Ho! ho! ho! ho! ho!

They laughed for a half mile past a rest stop, Chester laughing hardest.

"Hahhh hah hah...Okay! I got mine! That's what I needed, thank you. Now then, the reason I asked that was because it just dawned on me that you all are comin' from a different era, another erotic time zone, so to speak."

Suzy stared at him curiously, encouraging him to speak.

"I mean, it just suddenly popped into my mind, being somewhat older than you guys, that maybe you hadn't experienced certain things."

Suzy jammed him in the ribs. "Hey c'mon man, if you know something we don't know, let's hear it."

He took a big chunk of his sandwich, chewed, sipped some water, tried to figure out a way of talking about fucking, making love without condoms.

"Well, I guess I'm goin' to have to address this to the guys, because the lady has already experienced non-condomed loving."

"Include me in," Suzy said dryly, "cause I was so crazed at the time, I thought the guy had a rubber on."

"Okay, well then, I guess this is for everybody."

It was going well, they were sorting out positions, putting the layers together. He was going to lay some history on them, some of it good, some of it terrible. Maybe he was going to be the Man.

"Once upon a time, most of us did it without rubbers." No songs erupted, no university cynicisms, no smirks. He noted a strangely serious expression envelope each face. "In those days, there was a danger of the syph, the clap, maybe a bit of herpes, and definitely an unwanted pregnancy, but beyond that, I sayyyy, beyond that . . ."

He waited in vain for a beat, for a response that would've been automatic from anyone who had ever had the slightest connection to the Baptist church. Or The Religion.

"In those days, as the Arabic sayin' goes, we ate flesh, rode flesh and pushed flesh into flesh, and it was delicious. As everyone here knows, and I'm sure 'Doctor' Swanson can back me up, the genitalia possess some nerve endings that the rest of the body never knew anything about."

Marvin Swanson nodded enthusiastically.

"Now then, I sayyy, now then . . ." The Baptist preacher thang was missing the mark, he decided to head straight in. "We were into feeling more because there was more to feel. Some of the great fuck manuals of bygone days could be followed stroke by stroke because you could bring your thang out to half mast and lip stroke for a few beats. I think it'd be pretty hard to do that with a rubber on cause a lot of the nuances is lost."

He paused, to determine if he still had their attention. Four heads pirouetted in his direction. He still had their attention.

"Now I don't want nobody to get me wrong, I'm not suggestin' that rubberless fuckin' was for everybody, even back when. We had people, even then, who were carryin' round loads of unpronounceable shit. But it wasn't wholesale. The average person, or persons, could do it with almost no danger. You could go into a bar, a restaurant, a church, for God sakes!" He noted smiles creep onto Suzy and Marvin's faces. "Yeah, in church! As a matter of fact that's the only reason a lot of folks went to church. And synagogues."

Suzy laughed aloud.

"For some people it was like a low keyed fuckin' singles bar, without loud music. It was wild. Anybody could do anything with anybody they met, sexually. There were people who felt that they would rather get involved with you sexually than emotionally."

"Oh wowwww!" Bert exclaimed.

"Yeahhh, that's right!" Chester answered him, vaguely wishing that he had a taste of something stronger than mineral water. He made a quick survey of his audience. "But before I continue, let me ask one question, does anyone here have any coke, smoke or drink?"

Johnny, the driver, threw his head back and howled with laughter.

Evidently he was the only one who hadn't been in on the joke. He had taken the admonition to have "no smoke or drink" literally. His seat mates had considered the source. Bert held a cigar sized joint back to him, Marvin Swanson held a B.C. packet sized pack of cocaine and Suzy pulled a fifth of Myers out of her diddy bag.

"Woww! Whoa! I thought this was supposed to be a clean trip?"

"Yeah, Buddha, it's gonna be, because nobody's whose been doin' anything is gonna be drivin', that's the agreement. Right, guys?"

They all offered their unqualified affirmation.

"We kinda figured," Johnny continued, "that people might like to get high as we trip, but nobody drives high. Right, gang?"

Once again, they offered affirmative yeahs. Chester chose Marvin's cocaine snack.

"It's pharmaceutical."

"What's that mean?"

"That means it's about ninety eight percent pure, one toot'll do ya."

Marvin, with his medical training, obviously knew his coke. They were easing into Davenport, Iowa, before anyone else had a chance to speak. Chester made a mental note not to go for anymore of the "pharmaceutical." It could stimulate you to death.

"That's some mighty powerful stuff you got there, Marvin."

"I know. I only do maybe a line a week."

The driving, despite the official look of the drivers rotation schedule, seemed to rotate between Johnny and Bert.

"They don't really trust anybody else to drive their fuckin' van, really," Suzy whispered, doing a surreptitious number on her Myers.

They lurched into spontaneous sing-alongs of songs that he'd never heard of, some of them sounded like Black gospel songs with Anglo overtones. And, in between times, when he broached the silence with one of his favorites, they listened as though he were a latter day Belafonte. And he felt like one.

Beyond Des Moines, Johnny and Bert gave the other riders a chance to drive for short stretches, offering back seat advice all the way.

"Okay, Marv, let's not get any speeding tickets, okay?"

"Suzy, Suzy, how about staying on *our* side of the fence, honey?"

"Honey what, you brick brain?! What the hell does honey mean? You don't call Bert, Marvin or Buddha honey, why do you call me honey?"

"It's just a figure of speech for God's sake! What the hell do you want me to call you?!"

"Call me Suzy Franks, goddamit! That's my fuckin' name!"

"Okay! Okay! I'll call you anything you wanna be called, just stay on this side of the yellow line."

They spent miles exploring the nuances of linguistic sexism and racism.

"Of course, Jesse Jackson was the best man, no doubt about it."

92

"Hell, in that collection of run of the mill types, he stood out like a sore thumb. You think maybe that's why he kept using his thumbs up thing? As some kind of symbol."

"Well, you guys can say whatever you want to say, but I was for Dukakis from the first debate."

"But why, Marvin, why?"

"Well, for one thing, he was obviously the kind of robotic figure we need for these times. Jackson is almost a throwback. Don't get me wrong, I like the guy, personally."

"What do you mean by a 'throwback'?"

"The emotionalism, the appeal to people, that sort of stuff. That's old. We're in the Technological Age, machines run it, technocraft is the new state religion."

They good-naturedly hissed and booed his logic for a half mile, but allowed him to make his point.

"My point is that Dukakis is simply the best robot for this time. Now then, if he straightens the mess out as well as it can be straightened out then, I sayyy . . ."

A quick, wry smile at Chester.

"Then we can deal with the brother, with spirit feelings, hip slogans and all that."

Their arguments, discussions, monologues, dialogues, rotational orations delighted Chester, he hadn't had the opportunity to listen to "normal" white people ever.

Drugs.

"Of course, hard drugs should be legalized, decriminalized. What the hell is the point of slammin' some poor little shmuck in the can for umpteen years when we allow the liquor industry carte blanche and the aspirin industry and all the rest of the over the counter 'druggists'?"

"But Suzy, let's face it, honey . . ."

"Johnny, I'm gonna slam you in the balls if you call me 'honey' one more time!"

They plowed through hamlets in Iowa, seriously trying to

put South Africa in perspective.

"Of course, it's going to become Azania, no doubt about that, Chester offered. "The sin, shame and crime of it is that white racism in the world, including some colored racist help, I'm talkin' about the Japanese now..."

"Awww c'mon, Buddha, the Japanese have always been a little screwed up."

"That's racist, Bert."

"No it isn't, Suzy, it's stereotyping, and I feel that they've earned that title."

"If I can continue, without contrapuntal assistance..."

"Sorry, Buddha, please..."

"All I'm saying is that the psycho-history of white racism, not prejudice, but racism—held thirty million Africans in slavery well into the 20th century for one reason: money. And history and thirty million Africans, as well as their allies, people of African descent all over the Earth, will never forgive you for that, ever."

"Whoooaaa! Hold on now, Buddha!" Bert Candles shouted from the front of the van. "Hold on a minute! You can't say that we can be blamed for apartheid."

"Of course, I can. Any time you could allow that kind of inhumaneness to exist in your world then you are guilty of being a supporter of it."

He paused, feeling that he had been a little hard on the quartet, backed up a bit. "Don't misunderstand me, I'm not trying to lay a personal guilt trip on anybody here, I'm just tryin' to state a truth. And it's not only white folks I'm talking about. Millions of African-Americans allowed slavery to exist in their world and could've done something about it but didn't. As well as the Japanese. And the Israelis, who supplied apartheid with computers and guns.

"But mainly it was the white world, Russians as well as Germans, Spaniards."

"But Buddha, what about the African countries, places like Zaire, Nigeria, Ivory Cost, Zambia, Mozambique, and the rest of them who did business with the apartheid regime, who kept it propped up? What do you say about them?"

He paused to stare out the window, trying to collect his thoughts for a rebuttal. "The world is filled with sick people, always has been."

They stopped for thick wedges of apple pie and homemade ice cream deep in Iowa. The proprietors of the eight-stooled establishment insisted that they take a free pie with them. "This here's Molly, my wife, and nobody in Iowa bakes a better apple pie."

They were forced to agree.

MOVIES! Johnny Lambert the third, crossed lenses with Chester L. Simmons.

"Johnny, my man, we can't even begin to talk about an American movie industry yet, let alone a film industry, until all of the Americans have had a chance to strut their stuff. The American Indian has *never* had his point of view shown, by himself, the Asian-American hasn't been granted a show, and, as we all know, women and Blacks have simply been exploited. The so-called American movie industry, up til here recently, has been white protestant male in front of the camera and third generation Jewish white male behind the camera."

Suzy Franks gave him a resounding high five. "Sock it to the bastards, Buddha!"

Johnny Lambert the third reluctantly acknowledged that things were not perfect. "You gotta admit, things are changing. Look at Eddie Murphy."

"Fuck Eddie Murphy, man. I wanna see a Black Peter Sellers, a Black Ingrid Bergman, a Chinese Bogart, an Indian Lawrence Olivier, people who might actually expand the horizon of film to a point that's never even been considered."

95

They left the borders of Iowa behind, dwelling on the subject of love as they slid into Nebraska, under the cover of a beautiful misty rain.

They stared out at the random rainbows, carried on sililoquies as they drove through America's heartland.

Johnny Lambert the third directed his love affair from the first seat behind the driver, Chester L. Simmons, who felt quite awkward for the first ten minutes behind the wheel.

"She was the Mexican maid's daughter, for Gods sake! An impossible situation if ever there was one. I was fifteen and she was about twelve or thirteen, real Indian looking girl, no mestiza stuff here."

Suzy Franks caught Chester's eye and rolled her eyes heavenward with exasperation, the chauvinist asshole!

"We'd find ways to be on the same path on the estate."

"Estate?"

"We were staying with my grandparents, my Dad's parents, during this particular summer."

"Oh."

"We'd wind up sitting beside each other on the banks of the river, just dangling our feet in the water, staring at our reflections in the water. One afternoon we kissed, in the boathouse. The gardener, a Mexican guy, saw us, I found out years later, and he told the girl's mother and my mother. Two days later Elena was gone and my heart was broken."

Even Suzy looked sad.

"Just like that," Johnny continued, his voice suddenly fuzzy with emotion. "Just like that. I mean, it was so fuckin' crazy you know what I mean? I couldn't ask—what happened to Elena? Cause I wasn't supposed to care about what had happened to Elena. But I did care what happened to Elena. I still care. And I'm still tryin' to find out where she went, what happened to her."

They rode in silence for a couple miles, paused to gas up.

"Well," Bert started in, "this isn't about unrequited love, this is about love fulfilled to overflowing. As you all know, I'm gay."

Chester was the only surprised person aboard. He had had suspicions. How interesting that he and Johnny could be roommates. Well, it's a different ball game now.

"His name is Harry and, believe it or not, we met at a tennis match. Did you guy's see the last doubles contest they had in the quad?"

Marvin nodded enthusiastically. "Was he one of the participants?"

"No, he wasn't, he was a spectator, and so was I, and that's what made our meeting so funny. You know how it is at a tennis match, everybody's head is going back and forth? Well, after a few sets we discovered that our heads were the only ones not following the ball. We were looking at each other.

"It was a beautiful attraction. And I'm not going to discuss Harry because he's still in the closet, he wouldn't want to be discussed.

"But what I do want to talk about is what happens when two individuals get together who almost could be considered reflections of each other. The love almost becomes love of self. I think, in some ways, that homosexual love could possibly be the equivalent of a perfect love because it is so narcissistic. Is that the right term?"

"Who gives a shit, Bert, go on!"

"Well, what else is there to say? He's for me and I'm for him, one thousand percent."

Suzy Franks, nursing her bottle of Myers rum judically, nodded her head sagely.

"Okay, okay, okay, one failed romance with a Mexican maid's daughter, one gay romance. Guess it's time for the Judaic hour, huh?"

The van, which had become their 'spaceship' through pedestrian towns and prosaic fields, quietly settled into a sense of tension.

"Love? Well, it's kinda hard to get into that kind of ethereal feeling when your uncle is shovin' his cock into your mouth whenever everybody's back is turned."

"Whose fault was it?" Bert blurted out.

"Fuck whose fault it was, Bertie, it was happening and it blotted out a lot of stuff. I mean, how would you feel after your father's brother had been finger fucking you for five years to find some inexperienced shmuck tryin' to do the same thing to you on a date at the movies?"

"But, Suzy," Chester eased in, "we're talkin' about love, not abuse."

"And I'm talkin' about a time when you don't know any better. Let me talk about my love, okay. Is that all fuckin' right?"

"Hey, I was twelve years old and my uncle Morrie looked like a movie star and had a forefinger like a cobra. Yeahhh, I know about child abuse, sexual assault, all that. Uncle Morrie wasn't doin' any of that, he was making me forget the horrors of homework, Momma's scolding, Dad's impotent rantings. I'm sure you all know what messhuggenahs unitarian Jewish fathers can be, they bend so far over to be liberal, they may as well go on and become Orthodox.

"And there he was, my prince charming. I would've done anything he wanted me to do. When he said, 'Suzy, my, my, what nice tits you're developing,' and squeezed them, like you'd squeeze a melon in the market, for Gods sake! I almost fainted. I think I had a climax, I don't know."

"But c'mon," Marvin said, looking uncomfortable. "You must've come across some dude..."

"Hey fuckhead, whose turn is it, yours or mine?"

"Thank you. He spoiled me, needless to say. The first time

98

he jammed his cock in my face I thought I'd choke on it. But I didn't. And the first time he gave it to me from the rear I thought he was splitting me open, but he didn't and I was spoiled. I never hated him. I always loved him and I love him til this day because he knew what I wanted and he gave it to me, which is something that nobody had ever done."

"But, Suzy," Bert said quietly, "he was simply using you for his own gratifications."

"And that's exactly what I wanted," she answered quickly. "That's exactly what I wanted."

They were silent for miles. Suzy gradually leaned against Chester's shoulder. He circled her shoulders with his arm, snuggled her against his chest.

"God, you don't know how much I hated that man." She gritted the words out, too hurt for more tears.

Another rest stop, more sandwiches, a change of drivers, Chester's love story.

"I mean, it would've been damned near impossible to explain what we saw in each other. She was stacked stone to the bone, that much is certain, and there were a whole bunch of fish who wanted to swim in those waters. And a whole lot of 'em had, but that didn't bother me. She was what you might call a quintessence of ignunt behavior."

"A what?"

"I have to lapse into Black English, you dig, to try to explain Josie. She was ignunt. That doesn't mean that she was dumb or stupid. She was ignunt."

He took note of the furrowed white brows near him.

"She was shrewd, she could be cunning whenever that was called for, but mostly she was ignunt. Lemme give you an example: We'd go somewhere, say to a club or something and I could make book on her finding a way to act ignunt before the evening was over. She might wind up in a fist fight with the waiter. Or turn the table over if she didn't think she was being treated right. She got into an argument with the comedian in the Club Shebamin one night and wound up stealing the show from him.

"Poor guy, hahhh hah hah, he never knew what hit him. One minute he's doing one liners, you know, tryin' to pull the audience into his hip pocket, and the next thing he knows, Josie is all over him. She did more without a mike than he did with one."

"I kinda see what you mean't about ignorant now."

"No, Marvin, I said *ignunt*. There's a big difference. Life with Josie was hot, I think that's why they nicknamed her Heatwave. No matter what she did, she did it with passion. If she hated you, she hated you so fiercely that she'd make you hide if you saw her walking down the street. And if she loved you, well, you were very very well loved."

"You guys get a divorce?" Bert asked.

Suzy, having listened to him talk about Josie and life in prison the night before, studied her finger nails.

"No, I killed her."

"You did what?!"

"I killed her. She provoked me beyond reason one night and I shot her to death. It's called a crime of passion."

Johnny almost drove onto the shoulder of the road, trying to look into Chester's face in the rearview mirror.

"And he did fifteen years for it too," Suzy announced, a tinge of pride showing.

"Buddha, you mean you've actually been in jail for fifteen years?"

"That's what the lady said."

"What was it like?" Marvin asked innocently.

"Being in jail? I'd never be able to put that experience into words, not spontaneously anyway. Well, first off, it's not one experience, it's many, many hundreds of experiences

100

every day. There are days, for example, when a weird kind of euphoria can close in on you, something happens that can literally make you forget where you are. And then, the following day, or the hour after the euphoria dies, it seems like the day, or worse yet, the night won't ever end.

"I've had nights that seemed to last 72 hours."

"Woww!"

"Yeahhh, sounds incredible, huh?"

"It really does, it really does."

Chester stared out at the Nebraska prairies, hating to talk about prison, but feeling at the same time the need to purge himself.

"I never really understood what bothered me about going to the zoo, until I went to prison. After my first full week in the pen, I clearly understood why the panther paced back and forth, why the lion just sits in one spot, staring at nothing, or why the monkeys screw endlessly.

"The same thing happens inside. For one thing, number one, everybody is neurotic and must be, if they want to survive. And of course, a large number become psychotic, or are already. And these are people that you get in lines with, people who sleep over your head, sit behind you at the movies, stalk you in the yard. During the course of my fifteen years I must've seen at least one hundred men who should have been in a mental hospital for the criminally insane."

Nebraska looked so fresh and green after the rain.

"There was this dude named Morgan something or other, who was doing triple life and had killed eight people during the twenty years he'd been locked up."

Marvin looked like he was ready to puke. Suzy's eyes glazed in fascination, repelled but turned on.

"No one wanted to be within ten yards of him because he was apt to do anything. He said that he heard voices. Big son of a bitch. Muscles, a weightlifter. He'd killed one guy by twisting his neck around like a pretzel."

"How did you cope with him?"

"I didn't, not alone anyway. I always, always surrounded myself with a few other people whenever he was near. We had to do it for self-preservation. To be really frank about it, I don't think ten of us would've been a match for him. The guy looked like Frankenstein and was just as powerful. The prisoners *and* the guards were united against Morgan. We kept hoping that the guards would find an excuse to shoot him, any excuse, and the guards were praying that one of the cons would stick a shiv in his guts."

"What happened?" Johnny the filmmaker asked breathlessly.

"Nothin', he's still there. When I got out he had developed a relationship with a maniac who was twice as violent as he was, and they were cheerfully terrorizing the whole place."

Marvin Swanson held his head in his hands for a couple minutes, trying to make a grip on the scene. "Damn, I thought prison was where people were sent to get rehabilitated. I really did."

Chester released a dry laugh.

They had an easier time with Reaganism and abortion.

"Shit! I always saw Reagan as a latter day minor league Hitler. He had a Masters in salesmanship. Lotta people seemed to forget that the guy had only been a shill for General Electric before he became the governor of California. And while he was the president of the Actors Guild, he would've been to the right of Hitler, a complete fascist."

"But how does that explain his appeal to the American public?"

"The American public—meaning the Anglo Saxon Protestant ruling force—has always been fascist. All you have to do is check out where the 'founding fathers' were comin' from."

Chester L. Simmons, Mississippian, hip dude from the joint, settled back in his seat, semi-stunned by the talk of these white, privileged members of their society.

"I think Raygun came along in just the way that it was Adolph Baby came along—the moment was exactly ripe: Damn near everything was at a down point, people were pissed, money was meaning less and less, the Japanese were stickin' boot to our asses, everything was out to lunch. And up pops Big Daddy!

"To really be honest about it, I didn't really see the fallacy of Raygun until I started listening closely to Gil Scott-Heron and reading David Stockman. After I read Stockman, I understood some things that had been puzzling me for a long time.

"How did he get away with it? A semi-literate, semi-awake public servant? It was easy. Look at what Daley did in Chicago, for all of the years he flim-flammed and bamboozled the electorate."

Twilight seemed to gently lure them on to abortion and euthanasia, after cold pieces of chicken and illegal bottles of warm Heinekin.

Johnny Lambert III: "My granddad had himself killed and everyone knew it. The old dude had made at least a hundred speeches from his wheelchair: 'If I reach a point where I can't run my mouth, pull the plug', that was one of his favorite themes. And when he reached that point, Mr. Smithers, his super-loyal servant did exactly that, he pulled the plug."

"What happened to him?"

"What the fuck could happen to him? They subjected him to a couple months of soul searching and then released him with a lump sum of $50,000."

"But Johnny, aside from the special circumstances of a

rich grandaddy, what would you do about an ordinary person, a poor person, who was obviously gonna die, what about them?''

Johnny Lambert the third, quickly reviewing his personal view of euthanasia. ''Well, first off, I'd have to be honest and say that I've never had any idea of what it would be like to be poor, and dying, you know what I mean? But if you were on the verge of dying and didn't want to suffer, why shouldn't you have the right to go out?''

Suzy Franks dominated the abortion talks. ''Of course, we should have control of the right to give or to not give birth, otherwise we're just baby factories.''

''But Suzy...''

''But nothing, Bert, the pussy may be yours by right of seduction but the development is mine to determine. You dig where I'm comin' from, pal?''

They were caught in a small restaurant on the outskirts of Omaha by a beer 'n barbeque party.

''C'mon! C'mon in! You folks are just in time! It,s Wilbur Franklin's birthday and we're barbequeing a couple cows out back.''

The feast that followed gave them a conversation that lasted into Wichita, Kansas.

''Disgusting! I don't see how you guys could eat that... that...beef!''

''Suzy, honey...I mean, luv...I'd never be able to eat anything if I really honored the notion that everything has a right to life. I don't give a fuck whether it's a chicken or an artichoke, okay.''

The difficulties connected to the use of nuclear power was much less complicated.

''Nuclear power should only be used for peaceful uses. Any nation that manifested the slightest interest in developing nuclear power for anything but peaceful uses should immediately be wasted off the Earth by all the other nations on the Earth.''

''Wowww! Buddha, that sounds like a radical solution, if I've ever heard one.''

''One must think radically, at times, if one wants to survive. Let's call that African-American lesson number one.''

The hows hypnotized them, and caused Johnny to sing out his favorite arias, Bert to recite poetry by the stanza, Suzy to explain the shape of why things became elements of design.

''What?''

''Look at it: We have ideas, ideas are nothing but shapes in our minds, Gestalt bullshit to be sure, but still elements in our heads. And these elements must have shapes, they must become shapes, forms that we can feel familiar with, the White House...hahh hahhh...''

The discussion of Jew/African-American (''Why not Afro-American?'' ''Cause we're Africans in America, not Afros in America''), Asians/Latinos, seemed to take them to the outside of nowhere.

Suzy: ''I hate these little sections we push ourselves into.''

Chester: ''Then why should we talk about the Bauhaus style, as compared to the Wright style? Or the Hakayakawya style? We're not responsible for them but we definitely have to deal with them. What am I supposed to do, one day, when someone says, 'See there! That's a Franks building'!''

American racism wouldn't leave them. Chester L. Simmons made certain of that.

''Heyyyy, don't go gettin' your asses up on your shoulders because you're travelin' with a Black guy from Chicago to Taos. We all realize what the deal is, and that means nothin' has changed for the better and we all know it. If this van were stopped right now by the police, the person who would automatically get jacked up would be yours truly.'' He was forced to knock it off after five minutes of lonely raving because his arguments were indisputable.

The trip was coming to a close. They had made a navigational decision to slide straight across Kansas into Colorado, "just to look at it," and then slip down into Taos.

Johnny and Bert had been unobtrusively filming the passengers during the course of the interminable talk fests. "We'll have to have something to show the film panel when we get back. But most of the stuff we need is gonna come out of Taos."

Aside from their announced intention to have them participate in a few deliberately staged scenes, which never happenned, only Johnny and Bert seemed to know what the film that they'd received grant money to do was going to be about.

"C'mon now, let's face it, guys, Fellini didn't know what he was going to do, from day to day."

"Johnny, that was Fellini, not Lambert and Candles."

The filmmakers had to suffer for a few hours being called "Lambertini and Candlino."

Chester stared out at the lush countryside. Suzy gripped his hand.

"This is really a beautiful country we have, isn't it?"

"You better believe it." He patted her shoulder affectionately. Funny, he thought, I can remember a time when I would've been all over this young stuff. It didn't seem to work for Suzy. Maybe it had something to do with her history of abuse, but even prior to knowing about that, there was something that created a father-daughter bond, rather than a carnal urge.

Maybe I'm getting old.

He nodded off, closing in on the game he needed to make a hit out of California.

Chapter 5

They stood around in a small cluster at the bus station. Bert backed away, under "Lambertini's" direction. "We want to get a sense of intimacy in this, what we're sharing. We're seeing one of our favorite people go off into the unknown, to an uncharted section of..."

"Of for God's sake! Johnny, he's goin' to L.A.! That could hardly be considered uncharted."

They shared a laugh, exchanged handshakes once more. Suzy Franks draped herself around his neck like a python. "Suzy, Suzy, it's okay, sweetheart, everything's okay," Chester stroked her back.

A few curious types checked their scene out.

"I bet they think I'm Chuck Berry's younger brother or something."

They shared another strained laugh, Suzy held on.

"Well, kids, this looks like it, time to saddle up."

Bert handed the camera to "Lambertini" and joined Suzy's

coil on his neck.

"Heyyyy, hold on here, you guys tryin' to choke me or something?"

Marvin appointed himself spokesman.

"You've been a four year education, Buddha. You've taught us some things we never could've learned in school."

"Marvin, you've always known that you don't go to school to learn anything, you go to school for a degree."

He gently undraped the arms from his neck and started backing toward the bus that would take him to L.A., to his Avenue of Adventures.

"Buddha, you have my number 'n stuff, give me a ring when you get settled, okay?"

"You got mine too, let me know where you are, we'll exchange letters and stuff."

He popped into a window seat, waving goodbye to a couple tear-streaked faces, "Lambertini" cutting from one scene to the other, waving goodbye with his off hand. Nice people, really nice decent people, he thought, as he settled back for the three state ride to L.A. By the time this is over I'll be constipated for a year. He felt his stomach. It was disappearing, eaten away by days of eggplant sandwiches and no beer. Think I'll stick with the veggie number for a while, it doesn't make me feel all bloated and stuffed. Yeahhh, I'll lose some weight, transform myself a little, maybe do some exercises. He had pumped iron for a couple years at the beginning of his stay in the joint, but gave it up. Somehow it didn't seem to make sense developing a superman physique for other men to admire. Yeahhh, I'll get back on my program. He was heading into California feeling more positive than he had felt in years.

First thing I have to do is go to this halfway house.

Second thing I have to do is go where the money is. Third thing I have to do is make my trip to Mexico and trip from there.

It all seemed so simple. He woke up casting aside the dreams that were built on the lies he had told over the years. No, no more of that, I'm kicking cold turkey. The succession of people who occupied the seat next to him alternately bored, delighted, or left him feeling neutral.

The bores seemed to travel for longer stretches than all the others.

"Name's Roberts, Nathaniel Roberts. Been ridin' a while?"

"Yeah, since I left Egypt."

"Egypt, huh? I had some relatives livin' near there..."

Chester was forced to smile his way past the man's inane chatter. They were riding through Arizona: of course there would have to be an Egypt in Arizona, a Moscow in Idaho, a Cairo in Illinois, a Brazil in Texas. His joke had backfired. He closed his notebook, stuck his pen behind his ear and exchanged meaningless chit chat.

The delightful people only seemed to ride a short way, from one medium sized burg to another. Her name was Wendy Streets, she was 85 years old and on her way to an anti-nuclear proliferation rally.

"We've got to stop it now! Are you aware that Arizona has had so many nuclear devices tested here that they've lost count? It's almost as though the people here don't count. Do you understand what I'm saying?"

"I certainly do."

She left him with four homemade blueberry muffins as she departed the bus in Phoenix. "Chester, you look like a man who likes a homemade muffin."

California, two blueberry muffins left. He had milked the grapevine dry about California, about "El A," from the dudes in the joint to Ol' Steve, to Suzy, Bert, Marvin and Johnny.

Bert: "Awwww man, you're gonna have a ball, it's a wild scene!"

Chester: "Fuck the wild scene stuff, what do I need to do to make money?"

They were a little uncertain about the path to riches, none of them ever having had that necessity stare them in the face.

"Well, you're gonna need a car, I can tell you that."

"Yeah, the bus system is the pits."

The brothers in the joint had been a little more specific.

Marcus: "Yeahhh, dope, brother, that's the biggie on the coast. I know a dude who tripped out there with his hat in his hand and a year later he had a mansion, a harem and a Rolls."

He had considered the "underground method" during the course of the trip across the country, hadn't vetoed it from his mind, but had decided to play in safer arenas first, the pen still a fresh image. He knew the money was in Beverly Hills, the artsy fartsy scene was in Venice, the trendy restaurants on Melrose, scattered scenes here and there, but whose was Venice? Melrose? Beverly Hills? He hopped off the bus feeling new, liberated. The sun was gleaming and someone was going to help him get what he wanted.

He checked his duffel bag into a locker and bought a map of L.A. An hour later, after diligent study, he felt he knew east from west, north from south. Time to move out.

The heat outside the bus station felt tropical. He unbuttoned to the third button and slowly strolled west, absorbing. It was like most big city downtowns, busy, trashy, fast. Lotta Latins, Asians, hmmmm...Little Tokyo. City Hall. He flirted with the idea of going inside to have a meeting with the Mayor. He sat on the grass in front of City Hall, feeling giddy from the effect of the weather, the style of the people, the beauty of the women. Damn! Patcheye was right, they have sho' nuff got some fine sisters out here.

Yes, it was all new, he could take chances, do what he had been lying about having done. He could get off. Impulsively he spoke to a distinguished looking young Black man, a thought pushing a plan into being.

"Uhh, 'scuse me, youngblood?"

The man stutterstepped over to him, reaching into his pocket.

"It's all I can spare, man. I know how it is, I been there."

Chester stared at the dollar bill the man placed in his hand. Was it going to be this easy? He nodded thank you, and stuffed the bill down into his pocket, folding it around the two twenties and the ten.

Okay now, lemme see, I got two hundred and ten pinned into my drawers and fifty one in my pocket. That was a good omen, thank you, brother. He had simply wanted to ask the man a question.

"Where's the nearest employment office?"

Oh well...

He picked on a less affluent looking type, sprawled twenty yards away, a greasy haired Black man wobbling a toothpick around in his mouth. Chester made an oblique approach. "What's to it, home?" The greasy haired man looked at him suspiciously, and cautiously nodded. Chester squatted nearby. "Uhh, I just got in a couple hours ago and I need a place to sleep for a couple nights. You know any place?"

The greasy head frowned, wobbled his toothpick around. "You don't look like you need no place to sleep."

Chester was forced to admit, if a contrast in dress was going to be the determining factor, then obviously he didn't need a place to sleep. He stood up to leave. No greasy kid stuff for him.

"You might try over at the Mission, about six p.m. That's when they start takin' 'em in."

"The Mission? Where's that?"

"Down the street there, on Main. Uhh, lookahere, brotherman, why don't we put together 'n get one?"

Chester was already stepping before the end of the paragraph. That's all he'd need, to be popped on a drunk charge, vagrancy. He decided to check the Mission out, to make certain he knew where it was.

He prepared himself for the horrors of what he knew Mission life would be like. He joined the line at five-thirty p.m., duffel bag beside him. Yeahhh, it was mission life at its best: Skid row men, scabs hanging off of beaten eyes, noses crumbled into weird shapes, Black, white, brown, funky, semi-drunk, crazed.

A tall thin lipped ascetic slowly walked the length of the line, dismissing those who were obviously drunk or helplessly drugged out. "Sorry, Bob, we can't let you in tonight." A couple of the *men* protested, like children, throwing tantrums. The thin lipped man ignored them. He stopped in front of Chester, looked him up and down.

"If you don't mind me saying so, young fella, you seem a little too well dressed to be in need of our facilities."

"Don't let the clean shirt fool you, sir. I just got in town and I've got one buck between me and the sidewalk."

The thin lipped man stepped closer, obviously to smell his breath and look closely into his eyes. "Hhmmmmmmm, I see. Would you be interested in helping us serve the Lord's Supper this evening?"

Chester blinked involuntarily. "The Lord's Supper?"

"Yes, we serve at six-thirty p.m., as all the rest of the men in this line know. And then we have a half hour of devotion. We were accused, at one point, of using the food as a form of spiritual blackmail, so we decided to have devotion after supper. And the doors of the chapel are closed until devotion is *over*." The thin lipped man offered his version of a smile. It looked like a grimace.

Chester found himself with a white apron, standing behind a steaming table loaded with cheesy lasagna, day old bread slathered with government issued butter and an assortment of overripe vegetables.

The Lord's Supper.

He worked out a simple rhythm, spooning out the lasagna with one hand, passing out the bread with the other. The thin lipped man worked next to him, distributing the veggies.

"Uhh, brother Simmons," he whispered, "Let's not dig too deeply into the lasagna with each man, we have many mouths to feed and only a little lasagna."

"Oh, sorry 'bout that, Rev."

An hour later and the Lord's Supper was served, eaten and digested. Chester smiled, watching the men flee the half hour of devotion before they were locked in. He sat in one of the front pews, cynical thoughts flashing through his brain, as he listened to the Reverend Morgan I. Whitbred offer them bits of advice. "Every man and every woman here has a chance. Yes, indeed, every man and every woman here has a chance with the Lord."

Chester made a peripheral study of the people in the pews around him. A bunch of losers, if he ever saw one. The top layer consisted of profound alcoholics, the man (and two women) who would probably spend the rest of their lives drunk every day, and below them, a border line element that fluctuated from alcohol to pills to schizoid behavior and beyond.

Chester, trying to play pop shrink for a few minutes, surrendered his attention to Rev. Whitbread's homely little sermon.

"So, you see, my friends, I say to you, in conclusion, give yourselves up to the grace of the Lord and He will show you the way. Please bow your heads and join me in a moment of silent prayer."

113

Chester was tempted to throw his head back and laugh aloud. What the hell was any of this supposed to accomplish? Give a guy whose been drinking quarts of rot gut pluck every day, down on his ass in every kind of way, a slice of lasagna, offer him a little Christian speech and his life was supposed to be changed?

"Now then, for those who will be spending the night at the Mission, please check into the dormitory next door. Uhh, not that way, Frank, through the other door. Miss Smith will issue cot tickets. '

Chester watched the small group of men (and two women) shuffle out of the chapel into the dormitory. The Mission was a small compound: cafeteria, chapel and a fifty cot dorm.

They stank, some of them, they were bleary eyed, dirty, unkempt, goofy looking, some of them. But, he reasoned, there are probably as many nuclear physicists, doctors, judges, artists and whatever, as you'd find in the population at large.

Reverend Whitbred gestured for Chester to come with him. "Brother Simmons, will you join me in my office?"

Chester strolled behind the reverend, puzzled, a subcurrent thought about the possibility of the Reverend being a gay flashing through his brain.

"C'mon in, brother Simmons, have a seat."

Chester perched on the edge of an overstuffed chair, probably donated, his senses alert for wayward moves. The reverend slumped on a Danish sofa that had seen better days. The crusty look on the reverend's face had dissolved, the ramrod manner crumpled.

"Brother Simmons, if you'll look in the bottom drawer of that filing cabinet you'll find a fifth of excellent Scotch, please." They exchanged smiles; the reverend's smile was no longer a grimace. It hadn't reached the freeform stage, but it had softened. The reverend retrieved two coffee cups

114

from a nearby table, "just in case, Miss Smith happens to peek in."

Chester cooled his urge to speak, waiting for the reverend. He poured them three fingers of Scotch into their cups.

"If you will be so kind as to return the bottle to its hiding place."

Once again they exchanged smiles.

"Brother Simmons."

"You can call me Chester, if you like?"

"Thank you, Chester." They touched cups in a toast, took sips. It was an excellent Scotch. "Ahhhh, that really hits the spot after a long day. It's too bad our brothers in the dorm can't appreciate one of the finer things in life, in moderation." Chester nodded in agreement, his emotional antennae still up. "You're probably wondering why I invited you in here."

Chester answered with a shrug and a curious expression.

"Well, to put it bluntly, because I needed an intelligent human being who wasn't drunk or otherwise screwed up to talk to, you have no idea how lonely the business of saving souls can be."

Chester allowed himself to slide back into the chair, to relax. The reverend needed a little true confession time. Well, why not? Everyone needs somebody sometime.

"Brother...uhh, Chester, I've been in this business for twenty five years now and I've become, as they say, a shrewd judge of character. Midway through the Lord's Supper, I thought to myself, here's an intelligent person I can sit and have a drink with and not feel as though the world is going to come to an end."

"I heard that, Reverend."

They touched cups again, it *was* an excellent Scotch.

"It would be hard to explain to you how terribly depressing it can be to be surrounded by the dregs of humanity everyday.

And yes, they are the dregs, many of them. We can make an effort to feed them, talk a little about God's love, which most of them think is a crock o' crap."

Chester almost spilled his drink, amused by this new facet of Reverend Whitbread's personality.

"I know, I know, it is funny hearing me talk this way, but truth is the light of the world."

They shared two more cups of Scotch as Chester L. Simmons found himself on the receiving end of a story pattern that had started in a small town in Nebraska and was probably going to end on Skid Row in Los Angeles, or New York, or some place in between.

"I don't like to sound sanctimonious about it, Chester, and I know a lot of people take me that way, but someone has to care for the unfortunate, the oppressed, the sick, the drunks."

"But why you, Reverend, why you?"

"Because God wants me to do it."

Chester stared at the gleam in the reverend's eyes; was it the Scotch or evangelistic fervor? He decided to run a risk.

"But how do you know God wants you to do this?"

"Because He spoke to me."

Chester backed off, realizing that they were once again in the Valley of Fanaticism. He sipped his Scotch decorously.

"It was as clear a conversation as we're having here. He said, 'Morgan Jameson Whitbred, go forth into the world and offer hope to the hopeless, give food to those who are hungry, try to show them the way to Salvation'."

Chester suddenly felt tired and a little drunk. It never failed; whenever he listened to people who had been inspired by God to go through *changes* for the less fortunate he always felt tired, they always seemed a bit unbalanced when they started talking about why they were doing what they did.

"Brother Simmons, you look a little peaked, I think I've

116

worn you out with the Lord's words."

"Not really that, Reverend, I guess I'm just a lil' worn out period."

"I understand. Well, I've got to go and check on our guests. You may sleep in here on the sofa if you like."

"Appreciate that, Reverend, really do. Thanks."

"There's a blanket in the closet. See you in the morning. We serve the Lord's breakfast at six a.m. and then we have a half hour of devotion before we..."

"If it's just the same with you, Reverend, I'd like to leave my duffel bag here and start on a job hunt tomorrow morning."

"Yes, of course, I understand, Chester. Well, it's a pleasure to have had you aboard, no matter how briefly."

They clicked cups together and drained them in unison. The reverend stood up, dug into his pocket for a pack of gum, unwrapped a stick and popped it into his mouth. "Mustn't allow the troops to know that their general has feet of clay." He strode to the door, the crusty look and the ramrod manner restored, cranked off a jaunty salute and walked out.

Chester waited a few minutes before retrieving the Scotch from its hiding place, poured himself a generous four fingers and returned the bottle to its nesting place. He pulled the horsehide blanket from the closet, peeled down to his shorts and sprawled out on the sofa, his cup of Scotch on the floor nearby.

So, this is "El A,' almost too pleasant to believe. He made a determined effort, between delicate sips, to stay away from comparisons. "El A" wasn't like Chicago in any way, it was different, the pace was different, the people were the same, of course, but seemed different. The gangs were here, the casual viciousness of people that became epidemic in the late sixties was here but it seemed softer.

117

Maybe the sunshine has something to do with it.

He alternately sipped his Scotch and thought of his next move. Number one, a job, any job, but preferably one that will allow me to make some connections. And then let's see what happens. He drained the cup of Scotch and settled back, his head braced in his hands, thoughts melting into dreams.

Melrose Avenue, from La Brea to La Cienega. He hopped off the bus at La Brea not really knowing where he was, and not really caring, in a way. Several of the younger brothers in the joint who were from L.A. or had had the "El A" experience, had told him about Los Angeles. "There's lots of shit everywhere, Buddha, but most of the good shit is off in West L.A." Two of his better partners even got into explaining how the good shit of West "El A" differed from the good shit of the rest of the place.

"Now dig, Buddhaman, you got a lot of ground out there. Some of it might look like it's about something but it ain't. What you have to do is be able to distinguish between what is, and what looks like it is."

"First thing is the freeway system. The freeway system don't lead you nowhere; in a way, the only thing the freeway system does is take people back 'n forth to work. If you ain't goin' back 'n forth to work in 'El A', you're in serious trouble."

He understood, from the beginning of their "El A" expose, that he would have to strip a lot of the baroque trimmings away from their advice.

"Where would I go if I wanted to make a righteous money hook up?"

"Two places: Beverly Hills and West 'El A'. The beachfront scene is cool for body stuff, pussy 'n what not, but if you righteously want to get off into money—M-O-N-E-Y—then West 'El A' is the place to be, and Beverly Hills.

But what you got to understand is that Beverly Hills is that ol' fundy money, West 'El A' is wide open. Whatever you do, don't go to Watts, unless you want to tangle with a primitive drug scene, I mean...primitive.''

"Yeahhh, Buddha, them brothers be killin' each other off about shit that don't make no sense.''

Strolling west on Melrose, he found himself understanding what Brian and Marcus had talked to him about. It was a freak scene, that much *was* obvious, but it was a fake, faddish freak scene. The whole thing was so calculated and materialistic, he felt sick for a few blocks. So, this is what they had talked about?

"Yeahhh, Buddhaman, you gon' *see* some shit you never seen before in your life, them motherfuckers out there is live!!''

Even in the sunshine they seemed dead to him, the white ones like mannequins, the Black ones like idiots, the yellow ones like Eastern fools, and all the rest just simple-minded.

But he could see what the brothers had seen, it was LIVE, in a way that wasn't live in the East; maybe it was the technicolor. The hairstyles struck him as bizarre, but then they probably thought a fifty year old dude with a Dobbs stingybrim kind of odd too. He paused in a little funny looking cupboard to have an expresso. He had always dug expresso.

The street was full of expresso shops, wayward clothes stores, restaurants promising to serve the best food you ever ate, costumed people studiously fashioning themselves after the people across the street. Some people stared at him as he strolled past, obviously sane, curious, sober. He knew he was on another kind of Skid Row, but you had to be careful about this one, they might not call you bad names but they would take all your money from you. What kind of act could he put together, to get him out of the Mission?

He walked, the warm sun on his back, feeling ambitious, strong.

Dingaros popped up in front of him like a vision.

Busboy wanted.

The day time manager, a Marlene Dietrich-style blonde, thought he was joking. "You, a busboy, c'mon, git outta here!"

It took him a half hour to convince Marlene that he had to have this particular job if his place in the cosmic cosmos was going to be complete; he knew he had come a winner with his rap by all the sign points around her neck.

"But, you don't understand, we haven't hired a non-Latin to bus dishes here since the place opened!"

"Are you sayin' Blacks can't bus dishes?"

They exchanged challenging code symbols, the too hip Jewish princess and the hipper brother in deep need of a gig.

"Why don't we think parttime?"

"I don't have a place to live, I just got here, I'm struggling to hang on, is there a place where I can sleep here?"

She placed her hand on her hip and stared at him. No would-be Black employee had ever asked for anything but a salary and tips, if they came his way. This one was asking for a place to stay, on Melrose.

"Uhhh, Mr. Simmons, this is Dingaros, we are not in the habit of supplying an employee with living quarters."

"Then let's make an exception in my case."

He knew he had gotten halfway into her by her body language. Here she was, at thirty, minus the experience of knowing how a Black man in need addressed the issue of needing a job. She felt that he was just flirting, but why would he come all the way from Skid Row to flirt?

"You did say that you were living in a Mission, downtown?"

"I've had my first day and night here, in 'El-A' in that

120

place and I can't take it. If you don't hire me, I'll kill myself.''

"Well, we don't want you to kill yourself.''

"Then that means I'm hired?''

"Parttime.''

"What about someplace to sleep, change clothes?''

"Well, you could sleep in the storeroom. I don't think anybody would mind. But you'd have to get up early because that's when they deliver produce.''

"Sounds like a winner to me.''

"You know, this is a little unbelievable, in the 20th century, that we'd have a man like you, obviously intelligent, charming—yes, you are—willing to work as a busboy.''

"You must think Mexicans ain't shit, huh?''

She rolled her eyes at him as she beckoned for him to follow her.

Dingaros was almost a factory. There was a day shift and a night shift. Marlene put him on the night shift, to allow him to use the storeroom to sleep in.

"Where do I shower and shave?''

"My God, man! You want everything, don't you?''

He felt the emotional pulse, it would take him three weeks to pull her drawers down. He was going to have to do it because it was one of the things that would be expected from someone as bold as himself.

"Well?'' he challenged her to tell him where he was going to shower and shave, remain human.

"We can deal with that later, I don't live too far from here, maybe I can let you take a shower every now 'n then at my place.'' She brushed past him to show him where his locker would be, where he could get clean uniforms. She tried to ignore his erection. He smiled at her effort.

"Well, when do I start?''

"You could start tonight if you wanted to.''

121

"Okay."

She stared at him, frowning a little. "You really don't waste any time, do you?"

"I have no time to waste, I've done a lot of that already."

"Suits me fine. You'll start at four and it'll be all over at twelve a.m. The busboys on that shift catch hell, so look out!"

"I've been everywhere but the bottom of the sea, don't nothin' bother me."

"Whatever you say, Mr. Simmons."

"Call me Chester, please, I insist."

"Well, okay, Chester, but I'm warnin' you, the most important thing àt Dingaros is that you should be efficient and loyal. You start at four p.m., Manuel will show you what to do." He caused the muscles in her hips to flinch as she walked away.

The most important thing at Dingaros is that you should be efficient and loyal.

Bullshit. The most important thing at Dingaros was to get over.

For a few weeks working nights robbed him of his days. He literally dragged himself into the storeroom to sleep, night after night, brutalized by the work. Dingaros, this swank inter-continental restaurant, employed four busboys—two for days and two for nights. The daytime waitresses gave the busboys a percentage, the nighttimers kicked out a few bucks at the end of the night; they were stingy.

Chester went to *sleep* at the end of his third week dreaming of dishes. They talked to him, the glistening ones smiled, the dirty ones frowned and there were thousands of them.

The busboy's job was vital, underrated, underpaid.

He had suggested to Manuel, his mentor, after two weeks of shuttling dirty dishes to the kitchen, alternately washing

122

them, setting up tables, filling water glasses, sweeping, cleaning the toilets, vacuuming before and after their shift, that they ask for a raise.

Manuel stopped giving him one-on-one Spanish lessons and made an effort not to talk about anything but work. He was shocked.

"Chester, your estacion full, man."

Marlene came through with a shower after a week.

"You know, I've never thought of allowing a fellow employee to take a shower in my apartment."

"What's wrong with it?"

"I didn't say anything was wrong, it's just that I've never thought . . ."

"You never thought you'd have the Black busboy taking a shower where you take a shower, is that it?"

Marlene denied it. She denied everything. She denied that she was from Berlin, Germany, that she was a fake, that she loved Black men and white working on Melrose, she had had few opportunities to meet his type of Black man.

"What the fuck's that mean?"

"Well, let's face it, how many real men come into Dingaros?"

"Manuel is a man, Jose and Daniel, on the day shift, are men."

"Awww c'mon, Chester, those guys can barely speak English."

He teased her unmercifully, his back tortured and hurting from trying to do the work that two more men were needed for.

She began to make bold suggestions after he finished his weekly showers.

"Chester, aren't you forgetting something?"

He stared around her, on either side of her, ignoring her panties and bra. He was playing the cold game. She was not going to be the person responsible for him working like a slave and get some dick too. Never.

He was efficient, he was suave, almost too suave to be a busboy, people spoke to him.

"And how're you today, Chester?"

"Tired as a motherfucker, George, bussin' these fuckin' plates is a drag."

He even began to acquire a bit of a reputation, the busboy who told the customers exactly what was on his mind. Business picked up by three and a half percent. The owner, a Lebanese mafia type, took notice.

"Chester, don't you think that you're a bit out of line?"

"I can't see where I'm out of line, Mahood, I'm just being me. 'Scuse me, I got some dishes to bus."

There were times when the rhythm of the work turned him and his partner into robots, filled them with a weird euphoria. They hummed as they worked, ignored bad vibes, set a pace for themselves. Chester performed his duties as though he were a maitre'd of busboys. The summer was almost over and he felt that he knew all there was to know about the restaurant business, from the busboy level on up. He had lost his paunch lifting the baskets of dirty dishes and had saved a couple hundred dollars, sleeping in the storeroom. And he had made contacts. Lawyers, doctors, producers, professional people.

He had slipped a surplus Army cot into the storeroom, clipped a lamp onto a side beam, bought himself a small mirror, used the facilities. Marlene was becoming a serious problem but he kept her so completely out-foxed that sometimes she wasn't sure of who was chasing whom.

"Chester, are you gay or something?"

"I don't think so, why?"

"I'm just puzzled, that's all. I mean, you act as though I don't exist. You shower in my apartment, I've had you

124

over for dinner a few times."

"And I'm supposed to be so grateful that my dick will automatically jump at your whistle, huh?"

"You don't have to be so crude about it!!"

She had gotten in the habit of coming to the restaurant after closing, to have tete-a-tetes with him in the storeroom, perfumed, brushed, well cared for.

"Chester, I just can't make myself believe that you want to live like this."

"How am I living?"

"Well, like this. I mean, there's no reason why a man of your talents and charms shouldn't be doing something more than bussing dishes in Dingaros."

"Awww fuck you, Marlene! I'm so tired of hearing this shit I could puke. Everybody's always saying 'You oughta be doin' this, Chester' or 'You oughta be doin' that, Chester!' but no one helps me do a damned thing. I'm the one who winds up pulling the load."

"Sorry, Chester, I can understand how you feel."

"You can't understand shit. You can't even understand how *you* feel, how're you gonna understand how I feel?"

One night, after they had semi-argued for forty-five minutes and she was standing up to leave, he impulsively pulled her to him and laid a sidewalk kiss on her. He instantly realized his mistake. She was turned on now and determined to get something from him.

"So, you do have normal urges?"

"Get your ass outta here before I prop you up on one of these onion sacks."

"Why does it have to be on onion sacks?"

He gently pulled her out of the storeroom, through the back door to her car. "Good night, Marlene."

She stood beside the door of her car, her hands planted on her hips, staring at him in disbelief.

"You are really fuckin' something, you know that?"

"I know I am, I know that."

She popped into her car, fuming, frustrated.

He moved to a safe place just in case she decided to make a quick start and run him down. Hell probably has no fury like a woman put off.

It was time to make a move upward. He knew a little about the city now, where he was. They needed a waiter at Via Scampi.

"Well, Mahood, my man, this looks like my last week here, I gotta git on."

"Hate to see you go, Chester. I could give you a twenty cent raise, make you the captain of the busboys." Chester laughed all day long at the suggestion that he would want to stay on for twenty cents more and a funny title, "captain of the busboys."

He decided to go for a bit of overkill with Via Scampi, he knew that there would be about a ninety percent chance of him not getting the job if he walked in cold. "Morrie, I'm going up the street to the Via Scampi, to become a waiter, how 'bout giving me a letter of recommendation?"

The manager of Via Scampi, a short, swarthy Sicilian from New Jersey, stared at the five letters of recommendation from five of the most prestigious people in town. Two attorneys, a movie producer, the owner of Dingaros and a high echelon member of "The Family."

Chester concealed a smile, watching Tony Palermo's cigar wobble from one side to the other as he read the recommendation from Frank Manchetti.

"How do you rate a letter from Frank? From Manchetti?"

"I know him."

Palermo wobbled his cigar back and forth a few more times, Frank Manchetti's letter in his hands.

"You know, we've never had a guy apply for a job here

126

with five letters of recommendation."

"I'm sure."

"And in the fifteen years I've owned the joint, we've never had a Black waiter."

"That's unfortunate."

"This is an Italian restaurant."

"In *California* U.S.A."

They exchanged cautious smiles. Chester had decided not to take any of the ordinary shit from anybody. If they came up with something different, he'd give it some pay, but no ordinary shit. They'd have to save that for the chumps.

"You ever wait tables?"

"All my life."

Palermo pulled the cigar from his fat lips, the end gummy and chewed, and flashed Chester a big smile.

"You got a lotta fuckin' nerve for an old fucker, you know that?"

"I gotta lotta fuckin' nerve, period."

The job was his, starting day, this coming Monday.

"Don't worry 'bout nuttin', I'm here all the time, I'm the matree d', the cook, the accountant, every fuckin' thing, that's why this place is a success."

He was given a Via Scampi menu to memorize and given a tour of the establishment. Via Scampi served dinner from six p.m. to midnight. It was called "a class spot" by the congnoscenti, four waiters for twenty eight tables.

"So, you see, that's the way it is, Reverend."

Reverend Whitbred sipped his cup of Scotch meditatively. "I don't think we have a problem, Chester. Of course you can bunk down here for as long as it takes to get your act together."

"It won't be that long, I promise you. Now then, what're we having for the Lord's Supper this evening?"

"Lasagna, buttered bread and veggies. Oh, one more

127

thing...Kool Aid."

Chester smiled and clicked cups with the Reverend.

"Sounds ominous to me."

The reverend's thin lips tightened and his back stiffened for a beat. "Yes, I guess it would sound ominous if I were Jim Jones, but I'm not."

"Sorry 'bout that, Reverend, just jokin'."

"I know you were, Chester, I know you were. Come, let's feed the foodless. Here, chew this, it'll keep the guys from trying to drink your breath."

Monday afternoon. Tony had told him to come in early to "get in the groove," find out where everything was, check out a working kitchen.

"If you've studied your menu well, you know we do lots of seafood."

"I've studied."

"We got pasta up the ass."

"I checked that out, twelve styles."

"Believe it or not we had to cut out the veal 'cause my ol' lady suddenly found out how veal is created. You fuckin' believe that?"

"Tony, I believe."

Palermo studied his profile surreptitiously, gnawing on his cigar. "You wanna call me Mr. Palermo?"

"Ahh fuckit! You can call me Mr. Palermo when the guests are around."

"And you can call me Mr. Simmons then too."

"Okay, okay, okay, awready! Who gives a shit! Let's just give these bastards the best good and the best service they ever had."

Chester gave him the thumbs up salute and continued to absorb everything. His exterior was cool, suave, but he had a knot curling around and around in his stomach. He tried to focus on all the arrogant, egotistical waiters he'd ever seen in the movies, someone to focus on as a role model. He couldn't think of anyone. He knew he couldn't play devil-may-care-busboy in a waiter's uniform, he'd have to become someone else, create an original role.

"That's about all I can lay on you now, pal, you'll just have to get in there and sink or swim. I have to be honest with you, if you're not workin' out after a couple days we'll have to let you go."

"I understand."

"Okay, good. Sergio, Pasquale and Tony Jr. will be in at four-thirty or five p.m., they'll give you as much help as they can but basically it's on you."

"Tony Jr?"

"Yeahhhh, a chip off the ol' block. Thought I'd start the kid off where it really counted. He'll be in the bucks anyway, someday, so why not give him a taste of the bottom?"

"Makes sense to me. Now then, where's my uniform?"

He led him to a back room, the storeroom. Chester smiled at the familiar sacks of onions and potatoes. "Take your pick, you're here somewhere."

Chester made his way carefully through the rack. Burgundy bolero jackets, teardrop open white collars, navy blue cotton trousers, well tailored.

"No bow tie, Tony?"

"I worked in a bow tie, comin' up, it always made me feel like a monkey. And besides, Tony Jr. doesn't like ties, he says they're 'boor-shu-wha' or some shit."

Chester laughed aloud, the tension dissipated. It was going to be hard but at least he was dealing with human beings. "Great, no tie. Well, I've got a few hours before I start, mind if I chill out back here?"

"Make yourself at home, sleep if you like, I'll let you know when it's five."

Chester expertly lined a few crates up and laid back, exhausted already.

It was happening, he was living the fantasies he had lied about for so many years. How often had he claimed to have gone to a strange city and worked himself up from nothing? It was happening. He made a note to write about it.

Prison seemed light years away. It was strange. He felt, at one point, that the prison experience was always going to be riding his head, that he would never be able to make a move without considering how he had spent those past fifteen years. But that didn't seem to be happening. There were whole sections of time when his life seemed to have started from the time he was released and that all of the time prior to his incarceration was included, but not the spent time.

Maybe, he rationalized, it was his mind's way of adjusting to a maladjustment. But it was more than that, he knew that. There was this matter of celibacy that he was dealing with. Somehow, after being away from women for fifteen years, he didn't have the ferocious physical appetite that he thought he was going to have when he got out. Maybe it's age. No, he eliminated that one, not if the scene he had carried on with the two lovely ladies in Chicago was a barometer. No, it was something else, the will to wait until what he wanted came along. He made a mental note to touch bases with Marlene. He had been tempted several times to knock her off and get it over with but each time the little conscience-demon had whispered, "Don't do it, Chester, she's not the one."

Nor was the innocent middle aged woman from Guatemala that he had met on the bus one night. Or the bubble gum chewing Black woman that he'd struck up a conversation with in the laundromat. He didn't have a mold that she would fit but he knew that he would know her when she came on the scene. It wouldn't necessarily be marriage, bells ringing and all that, but she would definetely by the One he wanted.

He crossed and re-crossed his legs, trying to reposition a troublesome erection. *I would've been better off if I hadn't started thinking about women.* He used a prison learned trick of the mind to switch himself onto another track. *The trip in the van from Chicago to Taos was interesting. Think I'll try for another one of those someday soon.*

Marvin, Johnny, Bert and Suzy Franks, the halfway house, Chicago's lakefront, being able to open and close your own door, glancing through windows without bars, writing whenever he felt like doing it.

Scene after scene, frame after frame flashed through his consciousness, days and endless nights in the Joint, listening to escapes being planned, homosexual relations in the next cell, petty bargaining for cigarettes, black market marijuana, the idiocy of the prison system, of all systems.

California, "El A," the Pacific opening, warmth. He subconsciously flexed his hands into fists. *Mustn't forget the goal: Mexico, South America, get out of the country, do a Gypsy number for a few years. If anyone deserves it's, its got to be me. Fifteen years of my life for killing the love of my life.*

"Hi, I'm Tony Palermo Jr.!"

Chester felt totally disoriented for a split second. *Who in the hell could Tony Palermo be?* "Uhhh, uh, o yeahhh, Tony's son."

"Yeah, that's me, and you're Chester Simmons. Anybody ever tell you that you look like a Black Jap?"

"You mean Japanese, don't you, Tony?"

Palermo Jr. was a taller version of his father, minus the cigar.

"Uh, oh, yeah, I meant Japanese. No offense intended."

Chester made a careful study of the young man. This was going to be one of the people who would show him how to become a number one waiter?

"It's cool. Yeahhh, I've been told that. It's one of the reasons why some folks nicknamed me the Great Lawd Buddha years ago."

"Duh Great Lawd Buddha. Wowww, that's heavy, Chester. I mean like, you know, fuckin' heavy."

Chester sighed and stood up to stretch. Yeah, Tony was Tony, no doubt about which block he was chipped from. "Awright, now that we've gotten the heavy part out of the way, run the deal past me. Your Dad gave his version, I want you to give me the real deal."

Tony Jr.'s eyes lit up. "Please, have a seat."

Chester lowered himself back down onto the crates.

"Wanna get high?" Tony Jr. pulled a fair sized joint out of his shirt pocket and lit up, not waiting for Chester's reply. He took the joint when it was handed, more in the spirit of comradeship than to get high. The last thing he needed was a few hours of being out of touch with the basics.

Coff! coff! coff! coff! coff! "Tony!?" Coff! coff! "What the hell is this?"

"Just a little Thai stick with some Morrocan hash crushed up in it."

Chester took another deep hit and handed the joint back to Tony Jr.

Coff! coff! coff! "Thanks, pal." Coff! coff! coff! "Now then," Coff! coff! coff! "What's the deal with this waiting business?"

Tony Jr. took another expert pull on the joint, made a few random gestures and began to speak. "Okay, we got a fancy fuckin' I-talian restaurant here—good, good cookin', believe me. You wanna 'nother hit on this?"

Chester nodded, "No more for me," each motion seeming to lift him like a slow motion helicopter.

Tony Jr. placed the roach in a book of matches and tucked

it into his shirt pocket. "Okay, where was I?"

"Good, good cookin', believe me."

"Right! Okay, Mom does a lot of the cookin' or she's back there seein' that it's being done right. You ain't gonna get no gummy pasta in the Via Scampi. Dad will get into the kitchen too, if some of his pals come by..."

"Frank Manchetti?"

The marijuana sheen made Tony's brown eyes glitter. "You know Frank?"

"He was one of the people who wrote a letter of recommendation for me to get this gig."

"Heyyyy, that's great! Frank's a great guy. Any way, Dad will pop into the kitchen for something special if Frank or some other guys pop in."

Chester felt like floating up from the crate, his heart was doing a 6/8 cowbell rhythm and he felt as though he could wait on fifty tables. He felt powerful. "What I wanna know, Tony, is what do *we* do, the waiters?"

"Right. That's what I thought you wanted know. We perform. We perform miracles, we race back 'n forth from the kitchen with food that assholes have misordered and want to reorder, we smile and delight, we are charming, suave, representatives of Via Scampi, but we don't take no shit."

"I'm glad you said that!"

"I mean it! I threw a bowl of minestrone at a sombitch's head last year. It cost Dad a few bucks to *cool* him out, but would you fuckin' believe this dude had the nerve to tell me the fuckin' soup was cold when I put it in front of him?!"

"Well, was it?"

"Hell no it wasn't!! I burned my thumb picking it up from the tray. He was just an asshole. You get those from time to time. Look, Chester, what can I say? You seem like a bright guy. Go out there and pretend you know more than any sombitch who comes in here and everything will be

133

Okay, okay? Sergio, who can be a real prick, and Pasquale are gonna be on one side of you and I'll be on the other side, which means you really won't have but three tables to deal with tonight. So relax, pretend your I-talian, fuck it! You wanna 'nother hit before we go on?''

Six hours later, Chester stood in the men's room, counting a hundred and twelve dollars in tips. *No* one had even mentioned the tip factor. The actual work hadn't been too strenuous after all, they had two dudes from Mexico doing the dirty work, placing the table settings, pouring glasses of water, bussing the dishes.

He looked at himself in the mirror. There were bags under his eyes and his feet hurt, but he had made one hundred and twelve dollars in cash-tips *plus* the seven dollars per hour that Tony Palermo dished out. Things were looking up. The problem now was how to get home, to the Mission.

"Hey, Chester! C'mon man, bring your ass outta there, give the rest of us a chance to get in there 'n count our tips.''

Chester smiled his way out of the toilet, to be confronted by Tony Palermo Jr., Pasquale Franconi and a person he didn't know.

"How'd you know I was in there countin' money?''

"Shit! We all do it. Look, we're gonna run down into Chinatown for a late snack, you wanna come along?''

"I'll take a raincheck on Chinatown, but you can drop me off on Main Street.''

"Main Street, downtown? What's with Main Street?''

In line with his new policy, he decided to tell the truth. "That's where I'm living, for the moment.''

"Fuck you talkin' about man? Main Street?''

Three pairs of eyes swiveled across his face.

"Awwww c'mon, man you ain't no fuckin' bum, you got the makin's of a damn good waiter.''

"Tony, lotsa people stay at the Misson who are not bums.''

"Yeahh, I know, but not you, you're better than that."
The younger Palermo held his hand out to Chester, a gracious gesture. They shook hands. What about? "Look, man, I'll drop you at the Mission tonight but we gotta think about a decent place for you to bunk down."

"What're my chances of hooking up with a broad?"

"Who knows? In any case, you've gotta get out of the Mission."

They laughed and joked their way downtown, feeling upbeat, rich. The laughing and joking petered out as they slid off the freeway and headed toward Main Street. Chester gave directions to the Mission.

"Well, here we are, pal, Skid Row's finest." Chester shook hands all around before his exit. He walked slowly to the back entrance of the Mission, pleased with himself and happy to have a hundred and twelve bucks to play with.

Tony Sr. walked up to him on the second day, his familiar cigar wobbling back 'n forth in his mouth. "Well Chester, looks like you're gonna work out."

"I'm glad, I'm beginning to like the place."

"Oh, incidentally, I hope my kid's drug habit ain't causin' you any problems?"

"Tony, your son doesn't have a drug habit, he just likes to smoke marijuana and have a good time."

"Well, anyway, I hope he's not buggin' you.

"He isn't, as a matter of fact he's been very helpful."

Chapter 6

At the end of his second week he was beginning to understand why the government was so pissed off about people who could get by on undeclared income. By the third week, Tony Jr. had created a space for him in the apartment he shared with the other two waiters.

"We had to kick Sergio out, but he's a prick and we were looking for an excuse to get rid of him anyway."

"Really appreciate that, Tony, really do."

"No biggie, just have your three hundred dollars on the first of every month and everything will be cool."

It was falling into place nicely. He had a place to live, a nice hustle (what else could you call being a waiter?) and a bright future. He was managing to keep his libido in check, just barely.

"Marlene, you don't understand, I didn't come over here to seduce you."

"Well, why did you come?"

He thought heavily about the question. Why did he come over to her place? To let her know that he was doing well, that he appreciated the fact that she had helped him start out by giving him a chance. He felt grateful, she felt sexy. He decided to be as diplomatic as possible, no sense creating an enemy. This was a place where one of his famous lies could be used to the maximum.

"Marlene, look, let me give it to you straight. I think you're one of the most gorgeous creatures I've ever met and I've lusted for you in my dreams every night since I met you."

"You have?" She pouted her breasts out at him and rimmed her mouth with a bloody red tongue.

"Yes, I have but..."

Her face literally sank; what the hell was this dude trying to pull off?

"But I didn't feel that it was right to run the risk of infecting you." He knew he had touched the right chord from the way she blinked at him.

"Infecting me? With what?"

He cast his eyes downward, made his face look droopy. "Please, don't force me to say it."

She stared at him as he slowly backed toward the door. She gave him a sad little wave as he opened the door. "Goodbye Chester, good luck."

"Same to you, Marlene, same to you."

He hummed a pleasant little tune as he tripped to the bus stop, feeling good about himself. He had managed to avoid a sticky situation and remain unexploited.

The Via Scampi, after a wild month of fumbles and mistakes—"Waiter, did I *not* ask for Via Scampi special?" "Lady, I thought you asked for the special Scampi. No problem, I'll exchange your order immediately,"—became his playground. He dedicated himself to making money and the Via Scampi became his treasure chest. He was working seven tables now, strolling out of the kitchen with seven plates loaded on one arm, raking in tips like a gardener.

The restaurant was closed on Monday and he took no days off, not even when the fall weather became balmy and he felt like a young kid again.

"Eh Buddha, when are you gonna fuckin' take a day off, man, my Dad is beginnin' to think you're some kinda fuckin' workaholic."

"Don't worry about it, paisan', I got the rest of my life to take off."

He was aiming for three thousand dollars and his getaway date was set for the spring of the new year. He was twenty two hundred dollars short of his goal.

It was a slow evening, round about ten p.m., when she made her entrance. He couldn't think of a better word to describe her appearance. Several of the cognoscenti automatically applauded as she majestically glided to one of Chesters' tables, followed by three people; a woman and two men, obviously her employees.

Tony Palermo, Sr. removed his cigar as he made a respectful visit to her table. "Miss Ebun, I'd like to extend my personal welcome to you on behalf of the staff and personnel and everybody here at the Via Scampi. You honor us with your presence."

Chester made a quick, careful study of the woman, of the situation. He knew who she was, it would have been impossible not to know who she was; articles on her in People, Life, Opera Today, the daily newspaper. Ife Ebun, the Black woman they had nicknamed the Muhammad Ali of the Opera world, after she changed her name. "Somehow, it just never made a lot of sense for a woman as beautiful and Black as I am to have an Irish name."

Tony Sr. gave him a moment to get his act together by

passing menus around her table.

Ife Ebun, "love gift," from Greenville, Mississippi, by way of a thousand nights singing in dinky little joints along the way, church choirs, badly miked auditoriums, La Scala, the Met. He made an oblique approach to her table, took in the atmosphere she created. A dark skinned woman, cocoa colored, large firm African lips and nose, a big frame, the kind of build that Billie Holiday had, what used to be called "a stallion." He eased to her side as she studied the menu, Ben Franklin reading glasses perched on her aristocratic nose. Ife Ebun.

The rest of the people were suddenly overshadowed by her presence. The second echelon celebrities at table number four were completely chilled out, tables five and six gave evidence of feeling elevated by her proximity.

His approach was oblique, calculated. He was going to be a perfect waiter to the person a music critic had labeled, "one of the five great voices of this century."

"Good evening, Miss Ebun, my name is Chester L. Simmons and I'm going to serve your dinner this evening. May I offer you something before dinner?"

He flexed his leg, looked as relaxed as possible. Tony Jr. had given him excellent advice. "Don't get into that military stance bullshit, it makes people think strange things about the food, that it's being prepared by Army cooks or somethin'."

She turned to look into his face over the rim of her glasses. "Well, I see the Via Scampi has finally caught up to the spirit of the times."

He decided to smile himself past her comment. *This* was the one who was going to give him what he wanted, best thing to do was play the long game.

There was something grand about her, touched by a down home flavor. He recognized the quality that had given her the reputation of her being egotistical, "difficult." It was obvious that she was definitely in control, that much was apparent from the way her secretary, her accountant and her attorney looked at her. Tony Sr. eased one of her tapes onto the sound system, it was "El Amor Brujo." The opera singer and the waiter exchanged soft smiles, each of them recognizing the work.

"We'll have four Dubonnets, please."

"Brunette or blonde?"

"Which would you suggest?"

"My personal preference is brunette."

"Fine, that's what we'll have."

Tony Jr. and Pasquale had automatically slid in from both sides to cover his other tables. Tony Sr. rushed behind the bar to pour the drinks.

"Chester, do you know you're serving one of the greatest voices in this fuckin' country?"

"Tony, do you know she's being served by one of the greatest fuckin' waiters in this country?"

He settled into a rhythm, placing the aperitifs on her table. He wanted to do a service that she wouldn't forget, perform like an artist. After her second sip he strolled to her left side, his order tablet held behind his back.

"Are you ready to order now?" He watched her frown as she scanned the menu from cover to cover. She was obviously undecided. "I think I know what you want," he said, and moved to take the other three orders, the meat ball and spaghetti dinner, the sausage and peppers, the steak milanesa.

"And what is it I want?" she asked, as he returned to her side, the hint of flirtation in her voice. "El Amor Brujo" swept to a juicy whisper in the background.

"You want the shrimp marinara," he spoke in a low, seductive voice.

She glanced at the menu and nodded her approval.

"And what am I having with the shrimp marinara?"

"A small salad that I'll prepare myself, with just a dash of oil and vinegar."

Once again she nodded her approval.

He collected their menus and went to the kitchen to place their orders. Mrs. Palermo, usually a reclusive creature who hid behind pots and pans, snatched the slip of paper from his hand.

"Thisa one, I'ma gonna cook."

Chester moved easily through the cluttered kitchen to prepare the promised salad, feeling professional, on top of the moment.

The people accompanying Ife Ebun were obviously accustomed to being treated like second class citizens. The secretary was a mousy little woman who could've melted into the woodwork and not been missed. The accountant had papers for her to look at and the attorney had contracts for her to sign. Chester looked at her and the three people at her table through the kitchen door porthole. It wasn't unusual for stars to come to Via Scampi, for food or to be seen. And the reason was usually obvious after a few minutes.

Why did Ife Ebun come to the Via Scampi?

She came to see you, fool, Chester whispered to himself as he made his way back to her table with the salad he'd promised, his ego billowing behind him. He poured a thin dribble of Vouray into her glass as a companion taste for the shrimp marinara and received a luscious wink of appreciation in response. He was telling her that he liked her, that he liked who she was, that he liked where she was, with every suave move he made at her table and she was replying, saying I appreciate everything you're telling me. But none of this surfaced in words. She was the world class diva and he flattered himself, thinking that he was a world class waiter, but beyond all of the superficialities, there remained the fact that they were both Black and *that* genetic fact carried a code of its own.

He sensed when she felt the urge for another drop of wine and was there to pour it.

She dismissed her accountant after a brief exchange of angry words. "We'll talk about this tomorrow afternoon, Jack!" Jack the accountant slunk out. The two remaining employees looked nervous. Chester made a ghost move to her side, seeming to act as a calming agent for her anger.

"Is everything satisfactory, Miss Ebun?"

She stared at him. He met the residual anger easily, deflected it.

"Yes, thank you. Give my compliments to the chef. The shrimp were excellent."

"Why don't you do that? I'm sure she'd appreciate the compliment first hand."

Chester signalled to Mrs. Maria Palermo, staring in awe through the kitchen porthole, to come out. She did, after flinging her apron off and fluffing her hair out twice.

"May I present Mrs. Palermo, the chef."

The diva Ebun became the gracious, appreciative diner who could say, "I loved the way you prepared the shrimp" in Italian.

Chester took a step back to focus on the scene. Complex lady, one minute she could spit fire and the next minute she could be totally charming. He was pulling her chair back automatically before he fully realized she was leaving, it was the end of the first act.

"Thank you so much, Chester L. Simmons."

"It was my pleasure, Miss Ebun."

He glanced at the bill she slipped under the edge of her plate; he knew the tip would be large, but not a hundred dollar bill. He went into action, remembering his game. He stepped close to her and palmed the bill into her hand.

"Your performances are worth more than any gratuity you could offer me."

For a moment, the planet froze. Tony Sr. and Tony Jr. dropped identical jaws, Mrs. Palermo covered her mouth with surprise and Ife Ebun felt warm all over.

"I'll be doing a recital this Sunday evening at the Wilshire Ebell. Perhaps you'd like to come?"

"I'd love to."

"Maude, make a note to leave Mr. Chester L. Simmons a ticket at the box office."

"Yes, Miss Ebun."

Her Exit was as grand as her Entrance, minus one.

Chester, not missing a beat, turned his attention to his other tables, appearing to be calm, well ordered, but charged up inside. She had offered him an entry, an opportunity, and he was going to play it out to the max.

Tony Jr. floated over to his station, eyes glistening with a soft hashish sheen. "Buddha," he whispered, as he reached for Chester's hand, "you were absolutely fuckin' awesome."

Chester acknowledged the compliment with a feigned show of humility. Yes, of course, I was awesome. Why shouldn't I be awesome? Am I not the Great Lawd Buddha?

Tony Sr., Pasquale and Tony Jr. replayed the Entrance, the middle Act and the Exit of the Diva for two days afterwards, giving Chester a mystic status in the play.

Tony Sr: "You shoulda seen this guy! I thought he was doin' some kinda fuckin' dance for Christ sakes! As he moves back 'n forth to her table."

Tony Jr: "And then, to fuckin' put the icin' on the cake, he returns a hundred dollar tip. It was fuckin' awesome, I'm tellin' you, fuckin' awesome."

He smiled at their comments and continued to sharpen his knife. There was a lot to do before Sunday and he wanted to be ready. Ife Ebun was going to help him celebrate the end of his celibate state.

He stood off to the side of the lobby, his body swathed in an ink black three piece, pigeon blood-red shirt and tie. Tony Jr. and Pasquale, his roomies, had tried to force him into a more flamboyant costume, wear more jewelry, create a grand image.

"Chester, put on some stuff, man, do a peacock for her recital, c'mon!"

"Tony! Tony! Calm down, my friend, lemme run it down to you. I'm goin' to see the Diva, the Diva is not comin' to see me. Dig? I guarantee you, my super low key approach will be much more effective than trying to imitate a peacock."

The looks of admiration from the tux 'n gown set validated his outfit. It wasn't anything original, this ink suit number, he'd stolen the idea direct from the late Yul Brynner, who used to have black suits made by the dozen. "In a world where people are overstimulated, by television, by day to day living, by drugs, by whatever, the understatement is a powerful statement. The black suit is a powerful statement."

Chester flicked an imaginary bit of something from his lapel. The suit wasn't simply black, it was ink black, expertly and quickly put together by Frank Manchetti's tailor. "Frank, I need a favor. I have to have a suit by Friday evening, a good suit. Know anybody?" The tailor, a sewing dervish from Messiano, Sicily, was reluctant to do the work until he tripped on Chester's choice of material.

"No one, my friend, has asked for the ink in years."

"Ink?"

"That is what that color is called."

It looked like velvet but it wasn't. He made a mental note to ask the tailor what the material was made of as he marched to his third row, center aisle seat. The sister was looking out for him. He had never seen the diva perform and he wasn't the greatest lover of opera in the world but he felt confident of being able to appreciate a high note when he heard one.

The tux 'n gown set to the right and left of him offered him the patronizing smile they reserved for people that they assumed were "new members of the club." He returned their supercilious smiles with one of his own. They were curious. He had to be somebody to have a select seat in the third row, in their midst. He leaned back, enjoying their liberal discomfort.

The flashback made him shiver. "Madman" Jones had gone on a rampage in the yard, stabbing, biting, kicking, screaming. The cons were trying to put distance between themselves and the "Madman," screaming at the sharp shooters in the towers, "Shoot! Shoot! Kill the motherfucker!" The guards pointed their rifles at the maniac and laughed. They loved to see freak scenes, it made their boring jobs exciting.

The applause and pre-performance standing ovation jerked him back to Now. He disagreed with pre-performance standing ovations, philosophically. In his mind, no performer deserved applause until after they had earned it, no matter what their reputations were. But in this instance, with a vested interest, he joined the mob and stood politely clapping. He glanced at the program, remembering a three word sentence that an old con buddy named "Patcheye" had for events like this. "A bunch o' ol' white shit."

This "ol' white shit" had German names for the first half and Italian names for the second half. The lights went down and the audience focused on Ife Ebun.

He almost laughed aloud, from pure good feeling, looking up at this big, beautiful, cocoa colored woman decked out

146

in a Ghanaian caftan, singing songs from the German tradition. It was obvious, peripherally checking out the delight of his neighbors, that they didn't give a damn what she was wearing.

She came to the lip of the stage at the conclusion of the first half and bowed, ever so slightly. The gesture was cold, calculated, majestic. It said, There, take some of that home, into your sterile lives.

The audience bubbled with good vibes as they raced for shots of champagne and whiskey at the intermission lobby bar.

"I've never heard her in better voice!"

"God! She's better now then she was at Scolari in 1986."

"You notice the richness of her tones in the upper registers?"

"She sings a Wunderbar Deutsch."

Chester downed three whiskey sours during the fifteen minute intermission, high on his relationship to this outrageous women everyone was discussing. Midway through her singing of an aria from Aida, he felt the erection. He made an immediate effort to ignore this manifestation of his inner thoughts; it was, after all, a familiar event. How many times had his penis stiffened up as he leaned against the west wall of the penitentiary on a sunny day?

It wouldn't go away. During the course of one passage, he felt as though someone had placed an iron pipe inside his shorts. He tried to use prison spawned mental tricks to cool himself out. You're just horny, that's all, he rationalized. But he knew that he was bullshitting himself. He wasn't simply horny, he understood that. He was being turned on by Ife Ebun. And it wasn't her singing, it was her mouth. He stared into the crevasse that her mouth made, spilling glorious music out, and felt that he was making love to her. Her tongue warbling notes out made him close his eyes with pleasure.

Damn! Am I drunk or what?

"Huh?" the man next to him asked.

"I said, isn't she wonderful?" He flung himself back into reality, staring at the lips of the white seated on his left.

"Yes, she is."

He congratulated himself for not becoming extravagant, emotional, erotic.

You know a woman who sings that good has got to have . . .

She closed her eyes, clasped her hands at chest level and gave her emotions free play. She was Ife Ebun. She was a disciple of Sound and they had paid to listen to her. Her yoga instructor, the Indian from Benares who thought that money was an invention of the Ego, had told her, "Be careful of your voice; remember, Sound is the First Mood." There were times when the Sound made her feel like screaming, or crying. Or having an orgasm. It *had* happened a few times. It happened in Scolari in 1986.

They were at the end of the program and she had just gotten started. They were asking her to sing a few more lieder and she was just getting warmed up to sing another hour. But that was the name of the business, leave them yearning for more.

Chester stood, slumping slightly to conceal his reaction to her singing, to her mouth. It all came out during the encore. He tried to analyze what was happening. She opens her mouth and I see my dick inside it. The thought embarrassed him. He turned to his left and smiled. He turned to his right and smiled. The thought didn't go away. On the long notes, when her tongue quivered inside her mouth, he felt its pressure. When she curled her lips into a certain kind of shape, in pursuit of a certain kind of sound, his urge went with the shape. The eyes, the lips, the shape of the tongue, the juicy red clitoris in her throat signalled to him, made him

148

feel hot, sexed up. He was almost glad when the final number was sung.

"Uhh, pardon me, sir. Mr. Simmons?"

"Yes, that's me."

"Miss Ebun asked me to give you this message."

Chester took the note form the usher, puzzled. *Please come to my dressing room, I'd like to speak with you, I.E.*

"How do I get...?"

"Please follow me."

He pulled his shoulders back and sucked his stomach in, wading through the bubbling crowd, trying to put something together in his mind. The backstage area was bristling with workers, privileged members of the opera club. Ife Ebun sat in a chair that looked like a throne, as she accepted flowers, congratulations, adulation. The usher left him inside the door, on the fringe of the wellwishers. He felt vaguely disappointed. He thought that he was going to have her for himself.

He took a glass of champagne from the tray going around, leaned against the wall to study the scene. It could have been a scene from a thousand movies: opera star triumphs, accepts flowers, grins, little kisses on both cheeks, adulation.

She spotted him and pantomimed, "Don't leave, I want to talk with you."

The wellwishers thinned down to four after half an hour. Chester made no effort to intrude on their worship time, he simply hung back and sipped champagne. Finally, there were three people in the room; the mousy secretary, Chester and Ife Ebun. She looked at him across the distance between them, her black eyes gleaming. "Well, Mr. Chester Simmons, I see you made it."

He nodded agreeably, pleasantly high from three intermission whiskey sours and three glasses of champagne.

"What did you think of the performance?"

He stared directly into her mouth and answered. "I thought it was very exciting."

She licked her lips and smiled. "Maude, leave us for a few minutes, will you?"

"You mustn't forget the Sheffield party, Miss Ebun, you're the guest of honor."

"Don't remind me of anything unless I ask you to, do you understand that, goddamit!"

Chester was surprised by the anger of her attack on the mousy secretary. Why come down so hard on the poor little woman?

"Yes, Miss Ebun," she replied and quietly closed the door behind her.

He maintained his distance, trying to remember all of the advice his womanwise con buddies had laid on him during his fifteen year hiatus. "Never approach a fine lady, make her invite you to approach. They're used to having people come up on them, fulla pretty words 'n shit. Be blunt and direct, go for the head, not the crotch."

"May I call you Chester?"

"My friends call me Buddha."

"Buddha?" She stared into his eyes, as though she were seeing him for the first time. "Yes, of course, that's a logical nickname for you. I like it. I'll call you Buddha also, unless you make me angry and then I'll call you something else."

He smelled challenge time. "No, you won't ever call me anything but Chester, which is my real name, or Buddha, which is my nickname."

"Well, whatever. Come have a seat near me. I'd like to talk with you."

He casually bridged the distance and sprawled in a chair near her. The flowers scattered around her throne, the perfume from her body created an atmosphere. She was a beautiful animal, a creature of moods, an extremely talented person and knew it. He felt the need to be cautious.

"Buddha, that has such an odd sound to it, to be addressing a person sitting next to me."

"Call me Chester, if it makes you feel more comfortable."

"No, I'll stick with Buddha. I like it."

They paused to sip their champagne. He felt no need to rush the moment, whatever was going to be was going to be.

"Buddha, tell me, what do you know about food?"

Hmmmmmm. She was throwing some exotic trick shit into the game. What did food have to do with what they were going to do?

"What do I know about food? Well, number one, I know that you'll get fat if you eat too much of it."

"And how do you prevent yourself from eating too much of it?"

"You discipline yourself, or you get someone to discipline you."

She seemed to be pleased with his answer. He was puzzled by her questions. She stood up suddenly and made a model's turn in front of him. He admired the curve of her pelvic area. "I'm five feet eight inches tall and I weigh one hundred fifty-two pounds, normally."

"And it's well distributed," he said slyly.

"My problem is that I can gain fifty pounds in a week," she said, ignoring his comment.

His puzzled expression graduated to half a frown. What the hell was going on?

"I'm going to be going to Europe next month and if I'm not careful, I'll blow up like a balloon in a week." He sipped his champagne, masking his impatience. She reseated herself on the throne-chair. "I was quite impressed by the way you served me the other night and I want to offer you a position on my staff."

"A position on your staff?!"

151

She smiled at the surprised tone of his voice.

"Yes, I need a nutritionist, someone who will make certain that I eat properly during my tour."

"A nutritionist?"

"Yes," she continued smoothly, "my European friends love my voice and they bombard me with goodies, which add nothing to my voice but do expand my waistline."

A timid tapping on the door diverted their attention. Ife Ebun gestured for him to open the door. Maude, the mousy secretary, stuck her head around the edge of the door. "Miss Ebun, the Sheffield party?" Chester involuntarily ducked as the shoe whizzed past him. It missed the target head by a couple inches. The secretary closed the door softly.

"Now, where were we?"

Chester eased back into his seat. "Uhh, you were talking to me about becoming your nutritionist."

"Yes, my nutritionist for the European tour. You'll be paid a weekly salary, of course, and your accommodations will be taken care of."

"Let's be a bit more explicit. Is this a permanent position or what? What else does it involve beyond keeping you from stuffing yourself?"

Her eyes narrowed to slit briefly, she was obviously not accustomed to being questioned. "The position is for the duration of my tour."

"Can I get a contract making that stipulation?"

"Smart man. Of course."

"And the specifics of my job?"

"That too."

"And what, specifically, will my job be?"

"Well, as I said, making certain that I'm fed the right food. I may ask you to give Maude a hand, making reservations, that sort of thing. And I'm fond of massages, can you . . . ?"

He set his glass on the floor and walked behind the throne

to caress her shoulders and neck.

"Mmm...you have strong hands."

"What kind of salary are we talking about?"

"Two hundred fifty dollars a week?"

"I'd be a much better nutritionist for three hundred fifty dollars—three hundred fifty dollars and accommodations."

"I'm not going to quibble over a few dollars."

"What happens at the end of the tour?"

"Why don't we deal with that when we get to it?"

"I think it would be better for us to deal with it now."

"At the end of the tour, I will offer you the option of continuing or I will dismiss you. Fair enough?"

"Stick it in the contract." He gripped her temples between his palms and squeezed. She nodded in agreement as he released the pressure.

"Now then, if you'll be so kind, I have to prepare myself for a dull party before my secretary has a fit."

"I haven't said that I would accept the job."

"I beg your pardon?"

"I said, I haven't said that I would accept the job."

The eyes narrowed to slits again. "Is this some kind of game, Mr. Simmons?"

"No game. I just need a couple days to think on your offer."

"Are you aware that there are half a dozen people who would jump at the opportunity to accompany me on a tour?"

He shrugged eloquently. "So?"

"When will I have your answer?"

"Give me a number and I'll let you know by Wednesday."

"My secretary, who is probably waiting outside, will give you a number to reach me."

"Good. Enjoy your party."

He paused at the door, turned back to face her.

"Oh, two things; if I take the job you must promise never

to raise your voice at me or throw anything.''

"And if I do?"

"I'll kick your ass til your nose bleeds.'' He spoke with a smile and a hard edge to his voice.

They exchanged slitted stares before he left the room. He got a number from Maude the secretary and strolled out into the late evening air, looking forward to a European tour, his first trip outside the country.

Chapter 7

"Chester, are you fuckin' serious?"

"Tony, I *am* fuckin' serious."

"You mean you would hesitate to quit this job because of loyalty to me?" Chester had made a clever decision. Let Tony Palermo Sr. make the decision to relieve him of his job. Don't quit. It would mean he had given the man consideration, respect.

"Tony, I have to remember that you gave me a job when I needed one, okay? I mean, I can't just up and take off because some broad offers me a few months work."

Tony Sr. looked like he was going to swallow his cigar.

"Man, are you fuckin' outta your skull?! This broad is one of the top singers in the country, probably in the world. You'd be a nut not to hook up with her."

"You really think so?"

The owner of the Via Scampi gave him two weeks pay and a big hug. Tony Jr. gave him four huge hand rolled joints and a bit of advice. "Go for it Buddhaman, go for it."

He sat in the plush red seat in the VIP Lounge, watching Ife Ebun give another interview before their departure. Another interview, they seemed endless. He yawned, feeling sluggish after days of scrambling around to get his life in order to take a three month European trip. Passport, the right clothes for Luxembourg, an international drivers license, vaccinations, bureaucratic stuff. For the first time in years he felt a slight case of melancholia creeping up on him. He scribbled a hasty note to do a short story about the effects of melancholy. There were a few distant cousins and a wayward son out there somewhere but other than that, no one to care whether he dropped dead on this side of the Atlantic or the other. He had scribbled a bit to a couple friends he'd left behind in the joint and taken a moment to sip a little Scotch with Reverend Whitbred at the Mission during the course of his preparations to leave.

"Well, Chester, looks like you're on your way to bigger and better things, Praise the Lord."

"Yeah, that's the way it looks, Reverend."

"Great! Now then, would you care to stay for the Lord's Supper this evening?"

"May I be so bold as to ask what's on the menu?"

"Baked lasagna, french bread, veggies and Kool Aid."

"The Lord doesn't seem to like a lot of variety, huh?"

"Beg your pardon?"

"Uhh, nothin', just thinkin' out loud. Thanks for the invite, Reverend, think I'll have to take a raincheck on this one."

"No problem, we've got plenty mouths for the Lord's Supper. Glad you could drop by, glad things are working out for you."

"They are, Reverend, they are. They're working out so well, I'd like to donate a hundred dollars to the Mission."

156

He felt good about being able to make the contribution, it was, after all, for a good cause.

He glanced at Maude, the mousy secretary. He had developed a deep respect for her organizational ability and her capacity for abuse. It didn't make a lot of sense to him, that one human being should take any bullshit from another human being, but he had to concede that different people needed, accepted or wanted different things.

"Mr. Simmons."

"Please call me Chester."

"Mr. Simmons, you don't understand our relationship at all."

"Obviously not."

"Miss Ebun is under a great deal of pressure, always."

After Maude Thornberry gave him the equivalent of her "name, rank and serial number," they settled into what could best be described as neutral allies. He decided not to probe the murky depths of Maude Thornberry's warped relationship to Ife Ebun.

He yawned again. The interview was over, the first announcement for flight 689 to Luxembourgh was being announced and the diva was munching on a chocolate chip cookie. Where in the hell did she get a cookie from? He was beginning to have a cold blooded suspicion that his job as a nutritionist was not going to be an easy one.

"Well, Chester L. Simmons, or should I say Buddha?"

"Either one or both is fine."

"Are you ready to go to Luxembourg and places beyond?"

"I've been ready for the past fifteen years."

Crossing over he felt like a con who had suddenly been taken out of a "blackout cell," devoid of any sensory stimulation, into a world so filled with stimulation that he had to literally pinch himself in order to believe that it wasn't a dream.

Ife Ebun traveled first class. Her entourage, Maude Thornberry and Chester L. Simmons traveled first class. First class across the Atlantic spelled one big party.

Chester was taking his job seriously, after all he had demanded and received two weeks pay in advance and the right to have his return ticket in his possession. "Uhh, Ife?" They had also hammered out an agreement about what she should be called. "I'll call you Buddha, in affectionate moments, or Chester whenever I'm feeling serious and you'll call me Miss Ebun, at all times." "No, we're not going to pull rank on each other like that. I'm going to respectfully call you Miss Ebun in front of strangers, reporters and such as that and I'll call you Ife in more, shall I say, intimate circumstances? And you'll call me Mr. Simmons or Chester or Buddha in intimate circumstances. Okay, Ife?" The secretary was scandalized to the point of almost crying about the situation, to her Miss Ebun was a sacred designation, not to be tampered with.

"Ife?"

"Yes, what is it, Chester?"

"I don't want you to think I'm being small minded or anything, but I'd like for you to hand over that box of chocolate chip cookies." She flashed a tight little smile in his direction and handed him the box of cookies across the aisle. He flashed her a tight little smile of thanks and punched back into "How to Eat Well and Live Wisely." He knew that the "nutritionist" label was merely a cover for what he was planning to become, but in the interim he felt it would be to his advantage if he really found out what good nutrition was, just in case.

He placed the book in his lap after a few chapters and stared across the aisle at his employer. He hated to credit his fifteen years in the penitentiary for giving him the psychological insight to jump behind the masks that many people wore, to be able to pierce the iron veils that surrounded so many psyches. Yes, he hated to give the joint credit for that, but he had to. Being able to get the psychological uppers on another con could prevent a stab wound to the heart or prevent the degradation of being reduced to the thing-level by men who possessed the mentality of high grad monster morons.

Ife Ebun was extremely complex. He had seen all the evidence he needed to establish that. She shot from high to low and back, as easily as she hit the notes within the framework of her five octave ranges. This mercurial aspect of her personality seemed to spin off into several diverse areas. One minute she obviously felt like the Empress of Opera and a second later she was just simply a Black woman from Miss'ssippi who felt humbled by the richness of her talent.

She could be maddeningly illogical.

"Chester, don't you agree that if more Black people attended opera, it would no longer be considered a white art form?"

"I know a lot of people who've never considered it a white art form, it was simply a segregated form of singing."

"A segregated form of singing? What the hell does that mean?"

"That Black people, Chinese people, Indian people, people of color were not allowed to sing on the same stage with white people. I mean, let's face it, the Met didn't stay white as long as it did because there were no Blacks around who could sing Tosca or Aida or Carmen or whatever."

She rolled her eyes at him and didn't speak to him again for four hours. Her eyes were beginning to fascinate him as much as her mouth. They were black, an unusual eye color, he felt, for someone with her complexion. He had seen dark skinned Black people with grey eyes, green eyes, brown eyes, naturally, but she was the first black eyed Black person he'd ever seen. And she used her black eyes eloquently. They could literally sparkle when she was pleased or fire little cannon balls that blew holes through the people who displeased her. He loved them when he saw love in them, a picture of herself that she liked, a plate of Italian food. Her eyes swam in their sockets, gave her the appearance of someone who was experiencing ecstacy.

He turned away from her to stare out at the clouds above the Atlantic. How did that old doo wop song go?

"Life could be a dream, she boom she boom..."

A first class departure from Los Angeles, over the Pole to London for a hot minute and then a connecting flight to Luxembourg, the start of the tour, first class all the way.

First class meant the advance man from the Gregson Agency was traveling a week ahead, two countries ahead, to arrange for the best hotels, cars to meet the diva, level out the spots, browbeat the local promoters. First class meant that the opera star traveled with twelve pieces of luggage and was spared the horrors of waiting for her passport to be stamped by a bureaucrat in uniform. Chester and Maude were not spared that indignity.

"Your first trip to Luxembourg, suh?"

"Yes it is."

"Have a good time. Next please."

As the limo slid through the Luxembourg countryside, Maude made notes, Ife Ebun studied a musical score and Chester gazed at the picturesque landscape. He found himself smiling, delighted to be where his fantasies had so often taken him. How many times had he lied about hooking up with Italian countessas and doing incredible deals with international dealers? Luxembourg looked like an opera set to him. The neat little pastures wedded neat little towns and

160

the whole thing seemed to be inhabited by comic opera types.

"Fascinating, isn't it?" Mousy Maude had spoken.

"Yes, it is, makes me think of the 'Prisoner of Zenda' or one of those old MGM musicals with somebody yodeling from one mountain top to another."

He was almost shocked to hear the woman laugh aloud. "You hear that, Miss Ebun, that comes close to what you said the first time we came to Luxembourg."

Ife Ebun looked up from the score, over the rim of her Ben Franklins and snapped, "I didn't say anything like that. I said, I wonder if these fucking people have any collard greens, that's what I said!"

"Yes, Miss Ebun."

Chester turned his attention back to the countryside, no need to try to take matters beyond a certain point. He turned back to Maude a few minutes later, his curiosity aroused.

"Maude, uhh, Miss Thornberry, how many trips have you and Miss Ebun made to Europe?"

"Oh, at least forty or fifty," she mumbled, her nose almost buried in her note pad.

Ife Ebun looked up from her score and flashed a dazzlingly warm smile at her secretary. The smile bespoke of hardships shared, triumphs shared, comradeship.

Once again, Chester turned to stare out of the window. Fuck it...

If pressed for a description of the Hotel Regent he would've said, "old, funky, hip."

An endless procession carried their luggage up to the Queens Suite; Ife Ebun's twelve pieces, his three pieces and Maude Thornberry's three. The manager bowed and scraped them through the Suite.

"Ahhh, Madame Ebun, we have been awaiting your arrival. We hope you are pleased with your accommodations.

"If I'm not, Karl, I shall certainly let you know."

"Yes, of course, Madame."

Chester felt as though he were moving in the wake of a battleship, following "Madame" through the rooms of the Queen's Suite.

The suite was designed in an eagle shape, the head, body and tail in the center, two lesser apartments to left and right, the wings. Chester was assigned the left wing. He took note of the bottle of champagne, the large basket of fruit and the cake with "Welcome, Diva" on it as he passed through. He frowned at the cake, Ife Ebun smiled, Maude pretended not to see it.

The Manager bowed one last time on his way out. "If there is a need for anything, please call, I shall see to it personally."

Ife Ebun, making one of her customery switches, flickered one thousand volts of pleasant personality on the man. "Thank you so much, Karl, it's so good to be staying at the Regent again, if only for two nights."

As soon as the manager made his exit, Chester snatched the cake up and moved swiftly to his wing. "I'll hold onto this for safekeeping." The diva alternated a smile with a growl. He deposited the cake on his bedside table and flopped across the bed, feeling the effects of his first jet lag.

Luxembourg. He cupped his head in his hands and stared up at the ceiling for a half hour. Luxembourg. He folded himself off of the bed and went to stare out of the window at the clean streets, the well stocked shops, the well dressed Luxembourgers. These motherfuckers is rich. Two black faces swimming upstream, in a sea of white faces, caught his attention. He followed their movements until they disappeared. He felt an inexplainable sense of loss at their disappearance. Was it because they were Black like me? He turned from the window to face the cake at his bedside. Ife Ebun?!

162

He raced to the telephone.

"Miss Ebun's suite, please."

He listened to nine buzzes before the hotel operator plugged back in.

"Miss Ebun does not answer, sir."

"Thank you."

He strolled back to the window, gritting his teeth. He was feeling tired, agitated, irritable. Where in the hell was this woman? They had been in town a hot minute and she was already playing games.

He stood in front of the connecting doors and knocked three times. "Miss Ebun!? Ife?!" She wasn't there and half of the bottle of champagne was missing also. Damn! He knocked on the right wing door, the secretary's apartment. No answer. He turned the knob, the door was open. She wasn't there.

What the hell is going on here? He raced down to the lobby to look for the manager. "Uhh, pardon me, Miss Ebun went out to do some shopping and forgot to take her travelers checks, could you direct me to your main shopping district, please?"

The manager smiled at Chester's naivete. "All of Luxembourg is a main shopping district. I would like to suggest that you go to the restaurant C'est Le Vie, Miss Ebun usually goes there for her first dinner in Luxembourg."

The doorman hailed a cab for him and gave the driver directions in a language that sounded German but wasn't. He found out later that it was called Letzburger.

The restaurant C'est Le Vie looked like a two story castle and was obviously one of the swankiest in town. Chester stood patiently in the foyer, admiring the stained glass windows, the dark, gleaming wooden panels. The snow-white tablecloths. The maitre d' approached him as though he were a stale fish.

"Do you have a reservation with us, sir?"

163

"I'm meeting Miss Ife Ebun here."

The maitre d' looked vaguely uncomfortable. "Your name, sir?"

"Tell her Chester L. Simmons is here."

A few of the aristocratic diners turned to stare briefly at the Black American with the slanted eyes, as the maitre d' suavely strolled around a corner. He returned a few moments later and beckoned for Chester to follow him. First class meant no waiting in line, limosines at the airport, the Queen's Suite at the Hotel Regent, private dining room in the restaurant C'est La Vie.

He heard her laughter above all the rest the minute the door to her dining room was opened. The laugh could be added to the eyes and lips as a unique feature of her personality. The laughed boomed and shattered like plate glass being dropped piece by piece. He quickly counted six people, plus Ife Ebun and Maude Thornberry, who no longer had the appearance of a mouse.

"Come in, Mr. Chester L. Simmons, we were just about to have our fourth course. Come in, be seated!"

His eyes swept across the table, it looked as though a food war had been fought on its surface; the carcasses of four ducks, plates, a couple of rabbit dishes, rich sauces, wines, platters of goodies that he couldn't name were arranged across the surface. Ife Ebun looked at least ten pounds heavier and to top it off, the diva and the secretary were both semi-drunk. The six people sharing their food orgy were obviously rich, decadent, hedonistic.

Chester slumped into a seat that was placed behind him by an efficient waiter. Another waiter placed a bowl of soup in front of him. He waved it away. "I'll have a water glass of Canadian Club, if you have it?"

"Yes, of course, sir, immediately!"

He glared at Ife Ebun as she laughed, talked in a variety

of languages and accents and proceeded to take a bite out of everything within reach. Awright, Miss Ebun, if you want to get off into some real shit, let's go. He downed half the glass of Canadian Club and asked for a refill. Ife Ebun took notice.

"So, the cool Mr. Simmons does have a hot spot. Let me introduce you to some of my oldest and dearest European friends."

Chester gave up trying to remember their names after the third unpronounceable name had been bounced off his ears. "Pleased to meet you."

She had introduced him as "Mr. Chester L. Simmons, nutritional specialist," and received a number of cynical remarks in three languages.

"Please, everybody, speak English for Mr. Simmons' sake and whatever you do, don't say anything wrong or bad."

The dinner proceeded, the gayness hardened, the jokes were on those who weren't there.

"Ife, dahling, whatever happened to that marvelous tenor you had for a time?"

"Are you talking about Guisseppe or Juan?"

"Neither one...hah hah hah..."

Chester didn't care for their sense of humor, there was something vicious about it. He had the gut feeling that they would just as easily be talking about Ife Ebun if she lost an octave or fell out of favor with one of them. A pack of hyenas who preyed on the weaker ones. But he wasn't as much concerned with those factors as he was with Ife Ebun's gluttony. He shuddered as the word passed through his head.

He left his place and stutter-stepped behind her chair, the Canadian Club fueling his impulse. "Uhh, Miss Ebun, don't you have a concert tomorrow night?"

She seemed surprised to see him, gave him an affectionate pat on the shoulder. She was drunk. "Yes, of course, I have

165

a concert tomorrow night, that's why we're here.''

"Well then, if that's the case, don't you think you ought to be getting a little rest and relaxation?''

Her black eyes hardened for a moment, and surprisingly, she agreed.

"Yes, of course, you're right. Give me a few minutes to say goodbye to my friends.''

He stood by the side of her chair, a long way from being sober himself, after two tumblers of Canadian Club, but feeling proud of himself for having done the job he was hired to do. They had a delicate number going. He was certain that she knew he wanted her, but he wasn't at all sure of what her feelings were toward him. She was wealthy, she was young (thirty-five), beautiful, talented, well educated, but insecure and neurotic. It was hard to pin down what they were getting into, emotionally. He definitely wanted to make love to her; not fuck, make love to her. But he wasn't certain that she shared his sentiments. He had some indications that she was simply a woman who made use of men for a period of time and that was that.

She stumbled up from the table, blowing kisses to her 'dearest European friends'. One of her 'dearest European friends' called out, "Ife, dear, shall we have the bill sent to your hotel?''

"Of course," she answered, and draped herself across Chester's shoulders. He staggered out with her, followed by the secretary who exchanged a lascivious goodbye kiss with one of the women.

The maitre d' maintained his cool calling for a cab, as Ife Ebun, international star, slurred her English, telling him what a lovely place he had and how much she enjoyed dining in his establishment. "Soo good to see you again, Miss Ebun," he murmured diplomatically in response.

Everyone knew her, that gave him a funny sense of status.

166

Everyone knew her, which meant that they would soon know him. He felt a sudden surge of importance staggering up to their suite. You've arrived, Buddha, he told himself, opening the door to the Queen's Suite. Yes, brotherman, you've arrived.

Maude abruptly slid back into mousehood the minute they arrived at the hotel and slunk away with a timid sprinkling of her fingers.

"Good night, Mr. Simmons."

"'Night, Maude."

He made it to the French sofa before Ife Ebun came alive for the second act. "I want a night cap, I want some champagne."

"Ife," he spoke gently, "I think you've had enough to drink tonight."

She released her helpless hold around his shoulders and draped herself around his body, pouting her pelvis into his groin area. "Buddha," she spoke seductively, her black eyes on fire. "I want some champagne to celebrate my first night in Europe with you."

The kiss was probing, promising, deep. He undraped her arms and called room service.

"Very sorry, sir, it is already too late."

"This is the Queen's Suite, I'm ordering for Miss Ebun..."

"And tell them to send some hors d'euvres with the champagne.

"Did you say champagne, sir?"

"Yes, champagne and hors d'oeuvres."

"It will be up shortly, sir, thank you for your order."

He turned to watch her drop the dress she was wearing around her ankles, step out of it and head for the shower, the imprint of each gorgeous curve highlighted by a shimmering blue slip. He hesitated for a moment and made a quick decision, to meet fire with fire. He raced next door to his apartment, his urge deepening with each step.

He fumbled through his baggage for a pair of black silk pajamas, pulled them out, flew out of his clothes, raced into the shower, dried and cologned himself in less than fifteen minutes, dressed in his black pajamas and suavely made a re-entrance to the Queen's Suite.

Ife Ebun sprawled on the floor with a bucket of champagne and a tray of elaborately concocted hors d'oeuvres. First class meant the best at anytime of the day or night, immediately.

She was dressed in a red negligee, spaghetti straps straining from the weight of her full breasts, the material highlighting and caressing her body. The light on her came from a single lamp halfway across the room. Big, luscious woman, was the first thought that popped into his mind. Big luscious, beautiful, Black woman.

She pretended that she didn't know he was standing there, looking at her, as she popped hors d'oeuvres in her mouth and sipped champagne.

"May I join you?"

She looked genuinely startled for a beat. "Oh, Chester! It's you." She clutched her left breast, mimicking surprise.

"Who were you expecting, Michael Jackson?"

She released one of her booming, glass shattering laughs. "God, you are the strangest man!"

"Strange? Why strange?" He pulled a pillow off of the sofa and carefully sprawled on the floor near her; not too near, not too far away. Who knows, he thought, with her neurotic stuff going on, she might scream rape on me and then where would I be? Framed in Luxembourg. The headline blazed past his subconscious—"Ife Ebun, Internationally Known Opera Star, Raped by Born-Again Nutritionist."

"I don't know why I said strange, I just did."

"May I have a glass of champagne?"

"Yes, of course." She moved like a large snake, a python maybe, or an anaconda. "Would you like to hear some music?" she asked suddenly.

An inner frown was covered by a poker face. Damn! Is this the time for Don Giovanni 'n shit?!

"Uhh, yeahhh, some music might be nice."

A large fluid woman, how much did she weigh? One hundred fifty or so? Once again the analogy came into play. She did move like a large snake.

He was stunned to hear John Coltrane's "My Favorite Things" spill out of the radio.

"Wowwww! What station is that?"

"It's one of the three jazz music stations here in Luxembourg; they call it America's classical music. Isn't it lovely?"

He agreed, pulling her closer to him with greedy eyes as she sat down into a full lotus position. "You like jazz music?"

"Oh, I love jazz. I'd like to cut a jazz album someday."

He sipped his champagne, a mild headache developing from the mixture of Canadian Club and Piper Heidseik. Complex woman, full of contradiction-shit. "My Favorite Things" segued into a Phavia Kujichagulia performance. Fifteen minutes later, he turned to her, stunned into silence by the energy that had reached him.

"Who in the hell was that?"

"Phavia Kujichagulia. You don't hear much about her in the States. That's one of the reasons why I started coming to Europe so often. People over here seem to be much more open to our talents." After one full day on the scene, he didn't feel qualified to argue.

A brief announcement took them from Kujichagulia to an old Lee Morgan album, "The Sidewinder." Chester sipped his champagne, sprawled back on the pillow and dream-thought about his days on sixty-third street, on seventy-eighth street, in the Blue Note, at the Regal Theatre, in the joints on the southside of Chicago, the westside, the northside, the places where the fast people hung out, where the best music was played.

The sunlight bursting through the brocaded curtains and Ife Ebun's morning vocal exercises slowly stirred him to consciousness.

He felt the heat of her black eyes on the side of his face as the train carried them into the station at Brussels, Belgium. What the hell, he rationalized, every man has slept through at least one seduction in his life. And the whiskey, champagne and jet lag hadn't helped matters any. He was puzzled by her actions toward him. She seemed to have taken the whole thing in stride, but she was looking at him in a different way, with more respect. Maybe, he reasoned, maybe she thinks I deliberately planned it that way. He decided to play on that scenario and not do anything negative to his psyche.

The tour was tightening up. They were arriving in Brussels in the morning and her concert that evening at one of the largest concert halls in the city was sold out. They would depart the following day for an appearance with The National Symphonic Orchestra of Holland. They were scheduled for three days of rehearsal and then the concert, Modern Music by Modern Masters.

She had stunned him with her performance in Luxembourg. They had made her, designed her as the jeweled center piece in a jewel box of a theatre. The capacity was probably less than two thousand, the acoustics were pitch perfect and she had sang like an angel. He met her level gaze eye to eye. There was something opaque about her look, you could look into her eyes and not see anything. Or everything you wanted

170

to imagine.

He had chased people selling pastries and sandwiches away from their compartment from Luxembourg to Brussels. "But Chester," she whined at one point, "I haven't had anything since breakfast."

He felt sympathy for her urges but decided to play hardball. "Ife, look, you ate like a damned pig in Luxembourg, looks like you gained at least ten pounds. Okay? We're not gonna let you do the same thing in Brussels. You want to be able to wear all these pretty gowns you brought over here, right?"

She nodded yes, pouting like a petulant child.

"I've started a calorie count on you; you had approximately twelve hundred calories this morning, not including that double spoon of sugar and that half a cup of cream you poured in your coffee."

Maude the secretary looked up from her note pad. Her quick glance was filled with respect. What the hell was she always scribbling?

"Now then, the first thing we want to do when we get to Brussels is have a good Brussels meal. Where is the best restaurant in town?"

Ife Ebun's eyes rolled back in her head with ecstacy as she said the name, "Cafe Antwerp."

"Okay, that's where we go, you can splurge for at least six thousand calories. And the second thing we're gonna do is locate a health spa where we can work out for about an hour everyday."

"I hate physical exercise! I hate it! Making my body all sweaty! And besides, we're only going to be in Brussels tonight, we'll be leaving tomorrow afternoon."

"Good, we can trip to the spa in the morning." He felt good, powerful, in control. He, Chester L. Simmons, was telling one of the baddest singers in the world what to do. And she was liking it, almost. If only the brothers in the joint

171

could see me now.

The reception in Brussels was almost a replay of the Luxembourg reception, the car, the Hotel Bonaparte, the scene.

"Ahhhhh, Madame Ebun, eet eees soooooh gud to seee you again."

"Thank you, George, it's good to be back in Brussels."

The champagne rested in a silver bucket, the flowers and baskets of fruit were placed in strategic areas. There was no cake. She sent Maude to check out the concert hall. "Make certain that there is no dust anywhere. I almost ruined a performance with a sneeze the last time we were here."

"I remember, Miss Ebun."

Chester admired the efficiency of the Ebun operation. She would go to the theatre two hours before the performance and run through her music with an accompanist who had accompanied her on other trips to Brussels. The advance man was responsible for making certain that the chosen person was on the scene.

"Well, Chester L. Simmons, when do we eat?"

"Why don't we have something light sent up and then have a late dinner at the place you mentioned?"

"The Cafe Antwerp. That sounds wonderful to me, we'll go immediately after the performance."

He felt powerless to prevent her from gobbling four bananas and swiftly pouring three glasses of champagne down her throat. The concert was scheduled for eight p.m.; time to rest, put what was happenning into perspective. He sprawled on the bed in his apartment, stripped down to his shorts, indulgently scratching his balls, meditating on the incredible twists and turns that life was taking him through. Convict one day, "nutritionist" the next day. The coldblooded erection glaring at him told him that it was time to soft pedal the "nutritionist specialist," the food policeman;

172

it was time to go for the pussy again. Incredible, this women has hired me to keep her from eating too much and what I want her to do is eat me.

He drifted into a twilight sleep, one element of his consciousness focusing on the incredible good fortune he felt was happening to him and one element on his feeling of frustration with the circumstances he found himself in.

The liquid smoke of Ife's voice filtered through the door. She was warming up. What an incredible instrument that sister has. He raised himself on his elbows to listen. She rolled some of the notes of her songs around in her mouth like marbles, others she released like slow moving birds. Sounds like she's singing in Yoruba when she warms up. He called room service to order a late lunch for the three of them, fish and a salad.

"Yes, this is for Miss Ebun's party, Room 415."

"But we already delivered dinner to Miss Ebun's..."

He slammed the phone down. Damn! He struggled into pants and shirt and rapped on the connecting door.

"Come in," she sang.

He walked in, instantly cooling out the urge to rant and rave at the sight of dinner dishes scattered around the suite.

"Oh, I see you've already had your afternoon snack," he said, trying to be as sarcastic as possible.

"Yes," she answered sweetly. "I ordered something a little while ago. I was hungry."

He smiled at the pouting lips, the naughty little girl expression she pasted on her face. She was a beautiful sister, but he was beginning to see white beneath the black, the kind of neurotic stuff that most white women in America had always been privileged to indulge themselves in. Over the course of a few days he had found out what it was like to grow up black, pampered, privileged.

"I mean, I can never remember a time when I didn't have

173

everything I wanted. People automatically associate being Black and being born in Mississippi with poverty. I never experienced that; when my parents discovered that I had an exceptional voice, they sent me off to Madame Ragazetti in New Orleans, one of the great voice coaches in the world. I studied with her for four years and the cost was phenomenal. We weren't well to do, as they say, we were wealthy; not rich, just wealthy.''

"Well, since you've had your snack, I suppose you're ready to go to work.''

She slithered to him with four graceful steps, draped her arms around his neck and kissed him. "I'm ready to sing my ass off.'' She wriggled out of his arms before he got a chance to grip her buttocks in her hands. "You'd better get ready, Buddha, we should be at the hall in half an hour. I have to make certain that Thornberry's scouting report is on the money.''

He stood in place for a moment, the imprint of her body fresh in his mind. The frustration was beginning to get to him. She goes in and out like a fuckin' weasel.

"Oh, Buddha,'' she called to him as he returned to his apartment, "why don't you wear that gorgeous black suit with a white shirt.''

He bowed. "Anything for you, My Lady, anything.''

Chapter 8

He could tell at a glance that the Cafe Antwerp was the equivalent of Sardis in New York and that many of the people had just come from Ife Ebun's recital. He had to control himself to prevent himself from sneering at the glitzy crowd that surrounded their table. "Ooohh, Ife, you were divine, dahling, divine." The coocoo pecks on both cheeks, the super sophisticated chit chat, the air of elegance irritated him. He was suddenly nobody; maybe, to some people, a Black male version of Maude Thornberry. He didn't like the thought.

"And who, might I ask, is this adorable man in the black suit?" The question spilled out from one of the blonde streaked men at the table.

Ife smiled at Chester's discomfort. "This is Mr. Chester L. Simmons."

"How do you do? Wellington Fairchild the second here."

While trying to cope with the suave attentions of one of her "dearest European friends," he watched her devour a

175

large steak, a plate full of french fries, and a large plate of something that seemed to be made of whipped cream. She was blowing up before his eyes and he felt powerless to prevent it.

The crowd was slowly drifting toward the door, sweeping him along with the surge. "Maude, uhh, Miss Thornberry, where're we going?"

"To the Count's place."

The Count's place was a fifty room townhouse with a moat around it and uniformed guards patrolling the grounds. The Count, a tall man who resembled Bela Lugosi, welcomed them with an extravagant display of hors d'oeuvres, two open bars and a five piece jazz group.

Chester caught up to Ife Ebun, making her third pass over the hors d'oeuvres. "Ife," he whispered, "don't you think you've had enough to eat by now? You couldn't be hungry, you're just nourishing your insecurities." For a split second he thought she was going to throw her plate of fancy tidbits in his face.

"Why don't you get off my fuckin' back! I'm trying to have a good time and you're preventing me from doing that!"

"You didn't hire me to prevent you from having a good time but," he raised his voice slightly, "you did hire me to watch your diet, to keep you in shape, remember?"

"Well, you don't have to watch me any longer, you're fired!"

"Ohhhh, Ife, there you are. Come with me, the Count wants to show you his wine cellar."

Chester remained rooted to the spot, stunned. Fired!? The dirty rotten motherfucker. He felt like running up behind her and sticking his foot in her ass. Fired!? He was suddenly an invalid person who had no legitimate reason for being on the scene. Well, I'll be damned! He made a slow circuit of the half ballroom sized room they were partying in, steaming. The dirty motherfucker has fired me.

No one seemed interested in him any more, not even the "dearest European friend" who called himself Wellington Fairchild the second. He was beginning to feel embarrassed. He didn't know anyone in the room and he didn't speak Belgian, French, German, Italian or the brand of English they were using. He made an oblique approach to one of the servants.

"Say, pardon me, buddy. You have a taxi service I could call to get back to the Hotel Bonaparte?"

The servant fixed him in place with a dry, snobbish expression. "You want a taxi, sir?"

"Yes, a taxi, you ever heard of a taxi?" He was losing his cool altogether, becoming completely pissed.

"Yes sir, I have heard of a taxi. There is a phone in the foyer there."

He picked up the phone and suddenly realized he didn't know how to dial information or which taxi company he wanted to call or how to speak the language. He was surprised to find that ninety-nine percent of the people he spoke to spoke English. "It's a universal language, everybody in western Europe speaks English, except the French." He replaced the phone on the cradle and stood there, gritting his teeth and glaring at the phone.

"Can I help you, sir?" One of the maids, with a tray of drinks in hand, stopped near him.

"I'm trying to call a taxi but I don't know how to."

She deposited the tray on a table top, dialed, spoke in a language he'd never heard before (Flemish) and told him, "The taxi will be here shortly, I explained that it was for the Count."

"How much do you think it would cost from here to the Hotel Bonaparte?"

She did some rapid mental arithmetic. "I should think no

more than six or seven hundred francs."

He fingered the large, funny colored bills he had stuck in his pocket before leaving the hotel. Good thing my Momma always reminded me to take some money with me whenever I went out.

The taxi driver, recognizing a "new boy" on the block, overcharged him a hundred and fifty francs. He sat in the hotel bar, drinking gin and tonics for an hour, trying to figure out what his next move should be. Finally, sleepiness and lack of a plan B forced him to call it a night.

He knew that he'd have to trip back to the States as soon as possible. He was being realistic; with no income, no real game to play, not knowing anybody, he had no choice but to return. He dozed off thinking of the story he was going to be forced to tell the good guys at the Via Scampi.

He saw her silhouette framed in the blue light of dawn, and then she was under the covers with him. He felt that he was going to explode in her hand; such sensitive, tender fingers, a beautifully masturbating touch. Garlic reeked from her pores, the sour odor of champagne on her breath, sex oozed from her like a moan. She kissed him, the emotional heat in the kissing forced him to respond. They didn't speak, no verbal signals were exchanged, they simply felt. She was drunk. He came in her mouth the second her lips closed on the head of his dick and she came the second his tongue struck her clitoris a solid lick. He watched the sun ease up over her left shoulder as she mounted him. Greedy, experienced lovers, they played with each other for long moments before going onto other motions. After he nodded off for a moment, she eroticized him back to life by sucking his dick into her mouth and humming on it, as though she were singing a song. It was the sexual circus he had wanted for so long and when it was over, the bed sweaty and stained, cum frosted on both their thighs and at the corners of her mouth, he drifted off to sleep.

She was doing her scales when he woke up and two hours later they were on the train to Amsterdam. The gig was with the National Symphonic Orchestra of the Netherlands. They were going to have three days of rehearsal. The movements were fast with the diva, there were few margins for error. Or bullshit.

Maybe that's why, he thought, she's weird acting.

The gentle lurch of the train carried sexual overtures. He struggled to make eye contact with her; she ignored him, her attention claimed by the demands of the next program; Modern Music from Modern Masters.

Finally, unable to cope with her studious self-discipline, he interrupted her studies. "Look, Ife, since you fired me last night, I'm going to trip back to Luxembourg and go on home."

"I didn't fire you last night, you were irritating me."

"But you told me I was fired."

"So what? So now you're not fired! Now let me study, please!"

He settled back, nervously trying to pull it together. She was such an exasperating motherfucker. Okay, last night I was fired and today I'm not fired. I guess that means I was never really fired.

He made another mental note to cover his ass. In addition to having his return ticket in his possession, he was determined to get some guarantees about hiring and firing. He was going to become a union of one. He looked across at Maude Thornberry and dismissed the idea of creating a union of two.

She'd probably be the union scab.

The exit from the train station in Amsterdam had a split. They were met by the limo and chauffeur and taken to the right of the Damrak, the mainstream. He looked to the left

179

and wondered what the deal was.

The hotel Europa was a hotel dweller's dream. The phones worked (he called Sharlie in Chicago and left a message on her service—"Buddha here, in Amsterdam, just wondering what was happenin' with you 'n Edwina, sorry 'bout that, Ed), the toilets carried feces away so gently that he shat twice in one hour, fascinated by the gentleness of the plumbing. There seemed to be at least two people serving every room and there was nothing they wouldn't provide. This was, after all, first class.

The schedule that they had worked out called for them to rest for the first day and study. Ebun, who studied all the time, suggested that they go to her favorite Indonesian restaurant.

"I haven't had gulay kambing since I was in Amsterdam last year. Maude, do you recall the name of that place?"

Chester was feeling like a night on the town. Fuck this semi-neurotic bitch, let me get out and see what the deal is. Ebun held him close to her with fabricated strategems.

"Chester, I want you to go with me to our first rehearsal. I think it would be to your advantage to be seen with me."

And after the rehearsal, a late dinner at the Agung.

"What happened to your faithful friend and loyal companion?"

Chester took refuge behind the Agung menu, it was senseless to try to put a label on what they were to each other. Five minutes after they occupied a table, six of her "dearest European friends" joined them. Once again Chester became a "nutritional specialist."

He leered at her across the table. Why don't you tell them that you fucked the "nutritional specialist" til his nuts gave out last night in Brussels?

She ignored his leer and charmed her fan club.

Chester leaned back with an after dinner cognac, taking

180

the scene in. It was almost familiar now; wherever they went she was the basic center of attention and she loved it. He noticed the change that came over her whenever a circle gathered around her. Alone, she could be exasperating; with other people in attendance, she was charming, unpredictable *and* exasperating.

"Chester, we're going to do a little pub crawling, are you coming?" she whispered to him.

He made a surprise decision.

"No, I'm not."

The black eyes slitted and hardened. It was the first indication he had of her jealous nature.

"You're not coming?"

"No, I'm not."

"What if I order you to come?"

"Don't try it."

"Ife, are you coming?" One of her "dearest European friends" called to her.

"Chester, we'll discuss this back at the hotel," she snapped and made a sharp about-face.

What the hell was there to discuss?

It was 12:30 a.m. and the main street, the Damrak was lit like Christmas. Instinct carried him to the left bank of the city, where sin was expensive and regulated.

The first woman in the first shop window caught him by surprise, he thought that she was a store window mannequin, until he looked in on the second, the third, the fifth.

Well, I'll be damned!

In addition to the freelancers who swiveled past him, rimming their bloody red lips with lascivious tongues, there were the ladies of the windows. He crossed a bridge, turned back down the street and strolled past again.

Block after block, along the funky canals, women sat in shop windows, reading books (the Theory of the Leisure

181

Class), combing their hair, putting on lip stick, selling pussy.

He paused to study the notice taped beside the entrance to one of the shops, the "kum hours" listed the women on duty.

Wilma: 4 to 8

Greta: 8 to 12

Ingrid: 12 to 4

It made sense to him, if you had a favorite, you'd know what time to find her there.

He strolled along the canal streets, feeling perfectly at home, his hands dug into his pockets, trying to control a developing erection. I wonder if she's going to stumble into my room again tonight, this morning?

He liked Amsterdam, the funkiness of the city, the cross cultural polyglot flavor, the tolerant attitudes. He followed a couple hashish smokers for half a block, inhaling their exhalations.

Two a.m. He paused in a cafe for a shot of gin.

"Would you care for a brownie, mister?"

"A cookie? No, thank you."

The bartender laughed and explained that he wasn't simply selling cookies, he was selling excellent Dutch marijuana cookies.

A bright light went off in Chester's mind.

"Gimme a dozen of them bad boys."

It seemed to be all phones and trains. After she had cursed the conductor of the National Symphonic Orchestra of the Netherlands for dragging the tempo through the last three pieces, and received rave reviews from all of the major critics, they were on their way to Copenhagen, Stockholm, and Sweden. And points beyond. He was not quite sure when he wanted to give the diva a cookie, but he knew it wouldn't be long.

182

She forced people to cry and scream aloud with the magic of her voice.

"The Danes have always been kind to me," she said, casting her eyes down demurely in front of the interviewer from *Danish Life*.

Chester was seeing Europe from the plane of a verified atmosphere. It seemed to be trains and planes, but here and there, he had the distinct feeling of being in the Old World, and only in the Old World.

It had something to do with the sophisticated air of the scene, the casual way people seemed to take everything. The New World, in comparison, was frenzy and freeways.

Copenhagen, like Amsterdam, was a twenty-four hour town; a bright light was turned off here and another lit there. Someone had called the Danes "the Italians of the North" and after twenty-four hours in Copenhagen, he saw no reason to dispute the remark.

Once again they were placed on the Ebun three day efficiency schedules. The day of arrival was spent studying and checking out the hall, auditorium or theatre she was going to sing in. And eating.

"Chester, we're in Denmark, the fish is incredible."

The second day was spent honing the edges, making certain that all the props were where they were supposed to be. And eating.

And on the third day, almost as though it were a Biblical event, the concert. And then they'd be off to the next scheduled city, the following morning.

Maude Thornberry was proud of the operation.

"It was a bit sticky, at first, but now, with the advance man taking care of so many things, and an agency to fall back on, we are basically a self-sufficient unit, the two of us. All she has to do is sing."

Chester didn't bother to correct the secretary ("the two

183

of us.'') He was increasingly being drawn into areas that he wasn't hired to deal with, like keeping track of the Ebun luggage, making certain that her overseas shopping was properly mailed back to the States and a half dozen other "gopher" duties, in addition to his role as a "nutritional" bit.

He deliberately allowed himself to get behind her as they took a September stroll on the Stroget.

Look at that, her ass is beginning to look like two full moons rubbing against each other. He felt both frustrated and excited by her weight gain. He was frustrated because she was able to out smart him and gain access to fattening foods no matter how many obstacles he placed in her way. He had even gone so far as to force the hotel dining rooms to clear all deliveries of food through him. And he kept her in sight whenever they were anywhere close to pastries of any kind. And yet she was ballooning. Walking behind her he felt turned on by the classical Afroid proportions of her back, the strong thighs, the slender calves, the steatopygous bottom, the curve of her back.

Wonder when she's gon' break down 'n give me some more of that good pussy?

He had decided not to drive on her, to force the issue. She was just neurotic enough to spin off from a direct approach in a negative way. No, he had to wait for her, her number was called "surreptitious cunt," the kind of goodies that were dispensed under cover of darkness, between midnight and dawn, under the influence of alcohol. It was a delicate situation that left him feeling like a kept woman, someone who had to be available whenever the employer felt her head come down.

In a weak moment, Maude had confessed that he was the fifth "nutritional specialist" the diva had hired, over a six year period.

"Were the rest of them Black?"

184

"Well, I really can't get into that, Mr. Simmons."

"What's there to get into, I just asked if the rest of them were Black?"

After five minutes of badgering, she confessed, "One of them was almost black, I'd say. But I'm not really an expert on racial categories."

So, he concluded, I'm the first authentic, dyed in the wool Black man she's been close to in years. No wonder she's so neurotic.

After a few weeks on the road, he had pretty much pieced the puzzle together. Super talent from deepest Mississippi, sent to Madame Ragazetti's to have her pussy triple tongued by the Madam for a period of time, a virgin til she was twenty four.

"Sex meant nothing to me, I had no time for it, I was training my voice. It still doesn't mean a lot."

"What about love?"

"Isn't sex love?"

She was almost an idiot savant, she knew everything there was to know about music but life was an unexplored area. He felt tempted to ask her where and how she had learned to French kiss a dick so expertly, but backed off, afraid she would be offended. He had to be so careful.

Copenhagen become Stockholm and once again, late at night, bloated by food and wine, she slid in on him. He was ready for her.

"You want a snack, Ife?"

"You're offering me food?"

"Let's face it, all work and no cookies make Jill a dull girl."

Exactly fifteen minutes later she was howling at a cold Swedish night, as he labored to come between the two full moons.

"Ife! Ife! Don't make so much noise, baby, someone will

hear us!'' he whispered.

"I don't care! I don't care! It feels so fuckin' good! Do you understand me? It *feels* so fuckin' good!''

The emotions she aroused in him, this giant five-octaved diva, bucking and screaming obscenities under him, feeding his psyche sexual trick shots that kept his dick as stiff as a rod for a half hour. And then the climax, a melting of his core that forced animal groans from both of them.

During the post climax section she gobbled six cookies before he distracted her attention and hid them under the bed.

"Buddha, where are the cookies?''

"We ate them all, baby.''

"Don't lie to me, you hid them!''

The sounds of people in the hallway, pounding on his door prevented the argument from escalating. He hurriedly put on his robe and rushed to the door.

"Yes, what is it?'' he asked, peeking around the corner of the door.

The manager was red in the face with embarrassment. He stood, washing his hands, trying to find the right diplomatic words.

"Sir, this is a respectable establishment, never have we had such noise, such behavior...''

Chester was prepared to say the right words, ride it out, close the door. Ife Ebun appeared behind him and flung the door open, swathed in a sheet.

"And just who in the hell do you think you are?'' she roared past Chester's ear.

The manager chameleoned from lobster red to ivory pale.

"Ahhhh! Madame Ebun! I'm so sorry to disturb you but several people in the adjoining suites were, have been quite disturbed by the sounds coming...''

"How dare they be disturbed?! Am I not Ife Ebun, the singer? Am I not allowed to vocalize any time and anywhere

186

I goddamned please! Get the fuck out of my face!''

Chester stood to one side, blinking with surprise. The woman was full of contradictions. One minute she could be as humble as pie, the next split second, a raging bull.

She stood in front of the door, mumbling curses in five languages. And then she opened it, catching the manager and eight disturbed tenants by surprise.

"Get the fuck away from this door or I'll call the police!" she screamed. The people in the hall scattered.

Chester closed the door and tried to calm her down.

"Ife, Ife, I think everything's alright now, just be cool, I think everything's alright now..."

She paced back and forth in the room, loaded on marijuana cookies and ego, the sheet draped over her body like an elegant gown, shouting each sentence.

"The nerve of these bastards! To knock on my door..."

"Actually, this is my room, Ife."

"And I'm paying good money for it, goddamit! I'm paying for every goddamned thing and if I want to raise my voice goddamnit, that's what I'll do!"

And at the conclusion of the sentence, she released a high note that buckled his knees and shattered a wine glass.

"Ife! Baby! Honey, please..."

She pushed him aside as she stomped back and forth, pissed and loaded.

"I'll be damned if I'll allow myself to be treated like this! I'll speak to Gunnar Svensen the first thing in the morning!"

"But Ife, let's face it, there was quite a bit of noise being made..."

"And just tell me, Mr. Chester L. Simmons! Whose fucking side are you on?!"

"I'm on your side, sweetheart, I'm on your side."

"Then act like it! Now then, what did you do with these cookies?"

He made a snap decision to keep them concealed. She's already out of control now. There's no telling what'll happen if she had another one.

"Ife, I cannot tell a lie. I ate them to keep you from eating them."

She stopped pacing for a minute, to stand eye to eye with him.

"Why didn't you say that?!"

"I tried to but you wouldn't listen."

She draped herself around his body, the sheet acting as a carnal shroud, and kissed him. He loved kissing her, feeling the lush flavor of her strong mouth, the juicy play of her tongue.

"Ohhh, Buddha, I'm so sorry, I've been such a nasty one, why didn't you tell me I've been such a nasty."

He held her in his arms, enjoying the femaleness of her, her thighs, her stomach, her big firm breasts pressed against him. She brightened with a thought.

"Listen, I have a wonderful idea! Why don't we go somewhere and have a wonderful lobster dinner?"

"Lobster? Dinner?! Ife, it's four-thirty in the morning."

"Put your pants on, man, this is Stockholm and I know where we can get a lobster dinner."

The Kungsholm Restaurant didn't seem the least surprised to see the diva enter with a full length leather overcoat draped over a bed sheet. Chester looked slightly more respectable in pants, dinner jacket and plaid T-shirt.

"Gud morning, Miss Ebun, it is my pleasure to welcome you to the Kungsholm again."

"Thank you, Fredric."

"No broken plates this time, huh?" The maitred' said with a wink.

"No broken plates, Frederic, I promise you. I thought I was in Greece the last time I was here."

188

"Yes, of course, Madame," he answered solomnly.

Eight of her "dearest European friends" immediately climbed out of the woodwork and descended on their choice table.

The management of the Hotel Svenska made a formal request that the party and or parties in room 312 should vacate the premises as soon as possible.

"Well, lady, looks like we're being asked to leave."

"It doesn't matter, we were leaving anyway. But please be assured that I shall register a formal complaint against this *outrageous* treatment."

Chester shook his head from side to side, totally bewildered by the lady's warped sense of right and wrong.

After London, Paris, Rome, Naples and Barcelona, he felt like a grizzled veteran of the Ebun campaign. She had stopped singing for five minutes on one of London's most prestigious East End theatre stages to lecture a couple members of the royal family about the correct behavior at a public performance.

Some of the members of the audience applauded her for her action, including members of the royal family. Some booed her but most of them were too shocked to do anything.

For some perverse reason, the French loved her and she loved the French.

"You see, Chester, the French are artistic to the bone. That's why they're such assholes at times."

He couldn't understand it and didn't succeed with his plan to get her to go to a health club. Or to jog. Or to stop eating the rich cuisines of La Belle Francois.

"Why be in France and not eat?"

"But not everything, Ife, not everything."

Mousy Maude seemed to be watching the action from another planet. She took her abuse and kept on scribbling.

What the hell is she writing?

Ife sang in a theatre in Rome that made him think of the Cacsons, Christians, lions, orgies. And she made her music a reflection of all of that.

Sauces made a subtle entry. The sauce for the shrimp, the sauce for the pasta, the sauce for the oysters, the sauce for the fish, the sauce for the meatballs, the sauce for the sauce.

She pretended to be drunk in Naples and allowed him to lick Zabagbione from her labia mayora. The Neopolitans called her La Divina and tried to suck the life out of her with encores.

He knew he had had it by the time they got to Barcelona. It wasn't simply the sextet of wealthy European men pursing.

"Please inform Miss Ebun that Giovanni Giacometti is here and would like to see her."

"My name is Pierre Brasson and I would like for the diva to come to my home, to a dinner in her honor tomorrow evening."

No, it wasn't the men, it was Ife Ebun. Her life was too unreal for him, too flaky, unpredictable, crazy.

If she kept twenty-five hundred Frenchmen anxiously waiting for an hour, that was fine; but he couldn't take the mysterious fashion in which she dished out her pussy to him.

It was Brussels, it was Stockholm, at the hotel Svenska (a noisy scandal) a little taste in Naples, a lot of weird up close flirtation in between.

In Barcelona, he forced her to stroll on the Ramblas with him, to discuss his future involvement with her.

"Look, let's face it, I need more pussy."

He had learned how to talk to her, it didn't make a lot of sense to try to talk logically, normally.

"Oh?"

"Yes."

"Well, how much more?"

They strolled past lovers squeezed together on benches,

lovers talking nose to nose in sidewalk cafes, wall to wall lovers. He felt depressed, talking to a demented opera singer about something she had separated from herself.

"How much am I giving you now?"

"Oh, for Gods sake, Ife, can't you tell I'm joking with you? How in the hell could anyone measure pussy?"

"You seem to be pretty good at it."

"You don't understand. I'm trying to ask you to give me a normal love affair."

"Are you saying that what he have is abnormal?"

"Is there anything normal about making love every now and then, and only when you're drunk?"

He thought she was going to cry for a minute.

"Chester, can we stop for an expresso?"

They stopped for coffee in one of the hundreds of cafes that lined Barcelona's main street, the Ramblas. And she managed to have a couple croissants before he had a chance to object.

"Now then, what about his abnormal affair we're having?"

He sipped his expresso, feeling empty, defeated by the situation. How could you explain what real loving was all about to someone who had never experienced it?"

"Ife, look, what I'm trying to say to you is that sex isn't love. A man needs more than an occasionally drunken fuck. I need more than that."

"What do you need, Chester?"

"I need love."

She bit a chunk out of her croissant and spoke with her mouth full.

"But I don't love you, Chester. I don't love anybody, I love my music."

"I know," he replied sadly.

Chapter 9

After the recital in Madrid, attended by the creme de la creme of Spanish society, she slithered into his adjoining apartment for two hours of uninhibited sex.

He lay in place that morning, feeling drained, unsatisfied, after her exit.

What the hell is wrong with me? Here I am, running around the major cities of Europe with one of the most fantastically talented women on the planet, getting paid for it, and having a chance to get some of the leg too. What the hell is wrong with me?

He put it together that morning. She was giving him a case of the spiritual blahs. She was beautiful, she was skillful but there was no soul in what she did.

I may as well be fucking a hole in a watermelon, or something. I have to get out of this. Something more than a nut.

He dressed carefully, ran his words through his mind. He

193

didn't want to make an enemy or create a scene.

She was sitting up in bed, reading the reviews of the Spanish critics, eating her second breakfast of the morning when she invited him in.

"Ahhh, Buddha, you may approach the throne and kiss the royal hand."

He had to smile. After what they had done from two to four a.m., she was now offering him her hand to kiss? He decided to humor her by making a courtly approach, bowed and kissed her hand.

The Ben Franklin specs gave her a scholarly look that was offset by her left breast peeking over the edge of the covers.

"What do the critics say?"

"What can they say? I was phenomenal. I *am* phenomenal."

It would've seemed like sheer braggadaccio coming from anyone else but her.

"Yes, you're right, Ife, you are phenomenal."

He sat in a bedside chair, twiddling his thumbs.

"Well, what's on your mind?"

He stared into her hard black eyes and almost decided not to speak his piece.

"Well?"

"Ife, I don't want you to take this the wrong way or anything."

She folded the paper neatly and took her glasses off.

"You don't want me to take what the wrong way?"

He could feel tension developing. "I don't want you to misunderstand what I'm about to say."

"How in the hell will I misunderstand it if you don't say it?!"

He felt a sudden surge of pity for her, for the strong woman that people admired but didn't really know, considered a goddess amongst her peers, who was really an insecure

194

person who tried to surround herself with "dearest European friends" and food. She was obviously headed for the 200 pound mark in another couple weeks.

"Ife, this is the end of the line for me, I'm going to go on in a different direction."

She threw the newspaper on the floor and pushed the breakfast trays onto the floor. "You too, huh? What did you two do, get together and plot your desertion?"

"What're you talkin' about?"

"You know what I'm talking about, Mr. Buddha! You and that lousy little bitch that I pulled out of a whorehouse! Do you know what she had the nerve to tell me this morning? She had the nerve to tell me that she was leaving me and that she had a contract to write a fucking book about her experiences with me. She calls it, 'Travels with Ife Ebun.' What's your title going to be? Well? Tell me, goddamit! What's your title going to be, Chester L. Simmons! Why don't I write a book about you? I'll call it 'Helping the Waiter.' How does that sound to you?! Or maybe I could hire a ghostwriter to do it? What do you think about that?!"

He stood to leave. There was no sense trying to talk with her now, she had reached her familiar ranting, panting and raving stage. The only thing he'd ever seen that came close to it was a movie about Hitler, and the rages he went into when his staff tried to tell him the truth about the war on the Eastern front.

"I could write a dozen books about you scummy bastards! You're all the same! I take you in, feed you, show a little kindness and then you desert me! God! What did I ever do to deserve being treated like this!?"

He quietly closed the door behind him. He was already packed, he had enough money to take him through six months of Spanish living, if he wasn't too extravagant, and a return ticket to the States.

What more do I need?

He strolled through the hotel lobby and out into the streets in search of a stiff cognac, the diva's powerful voice echoing in his skull.

He strolled through the streets of Madrid, his hands jammed into his pockets, thinking of his next moves. I'm going to take my ass down to the southeastern coast, down to one of those small places that still has some semblance of tradition about it and get off into the writing life, seriously.

The thought of writing seriously sent chills through him. After all these years of flimflamming, it's time to get real.

He sat on the barstool, meditatively sipping his cognac, staring into his face in the mirror across from him.

Yeahhh, it's time, Chester, it's time. You killed the woman you loved because she messed with your stuff. You wrote an autobiography in the pen and tore it up. You've been making notes for months now and you know damned well the urge is getting stronger all the time.

He made a silent toast to Ife Ebun.

Thank you, you crazy ass super-talented motherfucker, for taking me into another turf, introducing me to another scene. It's up to me now, to make some more of my fantasies come true, it's time for me to become Chester L. Simmons, major league African-American writer.

He tilted the last drop of his cognac down.

What is the name of that little town that Chester Himes lived in? Alicante? Yeahhh, Alicante.

Well, if it was good enough for Chester Himes, it's got to be good enough for Chester Simmons.

He walked out of the bar, a determined look on his face.

Either I'm gonna be a world class writer or I'm gonna wear my ass out trying.

The Spaniards took note of the determination on his face and nodded gravely in his direction. They understood what it meant to make serious decisions.

Chapter 10

EARS RADIO THEATER

"Mr. Henry "Box" Brown"

TEASER

SOUND
(MUFFLED VOICES OF A RESTLESS CROWD, UNDER)

AUCTIONEER
(RAPID, RASPY SOUTHERN ACCENT)
Gentlemen! Gentlemen! Your attention, please!

SOUND
(VOICES MODULATE TO AN EXCITED MURMUR, UNDER)

AUCTIONEER

Thank you, gentlemen. This mornin' we got twenty choice bodies for sale and I don't want anybody to feel shy 'bout makin' a bid. Your money ain't earnin' all that much in the bank, may as well spend it on somethin' that you can use. Now then, let's git down to the business at hand 'fore the midday heat begins. Awright, Roy, let's bring that first one up here.

SOUND
(CROWD MURMURS UP, A SLAVE WOMAN CRIES BITTERLY, UNDER)

AUCTIONEER

Don't mind them tears, that's one of her tricks. As y'all can very well see, whoever gits this one will be gittin' double for his money. In 'bout another month or so, you'll be havin' a new field hand or a fine lady's maid. Now then, let's start the biddin', do I hear a bid of eight hundred dollars for this double deal?

VOICE #1

Eight hundred!

AUCTIONEER
Eight hundred! Do I hear eight fifty?! Nine?!

VOICE #2

Nine!

AUCTIONEER

Bid by Master Davis! Do I hear nine five-o?! Remember, gentlemen, you're gittin' double your money's worth. And if I'm not mistaken, it won't be the last time. To my experienced eye we got a prime breeder here! Do I hear nine fifty?! do I hear one thousand?!

VOICE #1

One thousand!

SOUND
(EXCLAMATIONS FROM THE CROWD, UNDER AND OUT)

AUCTIONEER

One thousand! Do I hear a thousand fifty?! Let's bid 'em in, gentlemen! Let's bid 'em in! Top flesh demands top dollar, strip 'er down, Roy...let the gentlemen look.

SOUND
(CLOTHES BEING RIPPED, WOMAN SOBBING UNDER)

AUCTIONEER

As y'all can see, aside from that lump o' future field hand or house maid, whichever it turns out to be, the gal ain't got but a few ol' whip marks, now let's bid 'em in! Do I hear a thousand one!

VOICE #2

Thousand one!

AUCTIONEER

Thousand one bid by Master Lee! Thousand two!? One thousand two!? Do I hear one thousand two!?

VOICE #1
(CALMLY)

One thousand two hundred.

SOUND
(CROWD RISES TO FEVER PITCH, UNDER)

AUCTIONEER

One thousand two! Bid by Master Davis! One thousand two!
One thousand three! Do I hear one thousand three!? One
thousand three?! Goin'! Goin'! Gone! Sold to Master Davis
for one thousand two hundred dollars. Take 'er down, Roy.
Awright, gentlemen, I'd like to die-rect your attention to the
next prize of the day. This mountain o' black muscle is named
Samson, works from before sun up til way past sun down
and can be put to stud in between times. Let's bid 'em in!
Do I hear fifty?!

(AUCTIONEER/CROWD, OUT)

HOST

Those were the sounds of a human auction being held in
Richmond, Virginia. The year was 1849. Those sounds and
everything represented by those sounds are the catalysts for
our story.

This story is a single illustration of the ingenuity and
desperation utilized by a man in pursuit of freedom. Henry
"Box" Brown was a real person. He, like many others, was
a slave who dreamed, schemed and planned to be free, at
any cost.

Why he chose to cramp himself into a box rather than
attempt to gain his freedom by some other method will never
be known.

What we do know, if the history of oppression teaches us
anything, is this: a human being's will to be free, by any
means necessary, is one of the most powerful forces on earth.

MUSIC
(BANJO SOLO, MAIN TITLE, HOLD UNDER)

EARS RADIO THEATER, a new adventure in radio listening, brought to you five nights a week; five nights of exceptional entertainment every week, brought to you by Ears Radio Theater.

MUSIC
(UP FULL, RESOLVE, THEN OUT UNDER)

ANNOUNCER

Our story, *Mr. Henry "Box" Brown*, by_____.
Our Star,_____.

(OPENING COMMERCIAL)

ACT ONE

MUSIC
(A PHRASE)

HOST

Our story begins on a warm day in March of 1849, in Richmond, Virginia. Henry Brown, occupation, slave, walks into his neighborhood general store.

Henry, confined by law to slavery, it owned by two men. His owner, Paul Carson, taking advantage of his skill as a tobacconist, rents him to a tobacco factory owner and charges Henry $25 a month for the "privilege" of allowing him to work. His body and salary belong to his masters but he has to fend for himself...these are some of the conditions under which he must labor.

Despite the fact that he has been a slave for all of his thirty

three years, there is an undefinable something in his eyes
that tells us that he doesn't think like a slave. He is small,
about 5'5" or so, muscular from years of handling heavy
bales of tobacco leaves and has one hundred and sixty six
dollars hidden in the lining of his hand-me-down coat, money
earned penny by penny over the years, doing odd jobs.

SOUND
(HENRY'S FOOTSTEPS ON WOODEN PLANKS
OF THE STORE'S FLOOR)

BOB YANCEY
(STORE OWNER, CONGENIAL, WHITE SOUTHERN ACCENT)
Well now, what can we do for you today, Henry?

HENRY
(BLACK SOUTHERN ACCENT)
Nothin' too much, Mister Yancey, a lil' salt maybe
and...uhh...a lil' snuff.

YANCEY
(SYMPATHETICALLY)
What's the trouble, Henry? You look like you got a ton o'
bricks on each shoulder.

HENRY
I kinda feel that way, Mister Yancey.

YANCEY
Your wife?

HENRY
(SADLY)
Yessir, my wife. Her master sold her down South. I didn't
find out 'bout it 'til yesterday, when I got my pass to go over
to see her.

YANCEY

She was owned by the Stovalls, wasn't she?

HENRY

Yessir.

(PAUSE)

YANCEY

Did you go talk to your master about buyin' her, like I told you to?

HENRY

Yessir, I begged him to...and he said he would. But he didn't.

YANCEY

Who bought her?

HENRY
(DESPONDENTLY)

I don't know, she was brought up in a batch that was being taken South to be resold. I'll never see her again.

YANCEY

I'd be lyin' if I didn't agree with you, Henry. Seems 'bout the best thing for you to do is ask your master to buy you another wife.

HENRY
(IN LOW, BITTER TONES)

I don't want another slave woman for a wife! Somebody that can be bought 'n sold!

YANCEY

Whoa! Take it easy now, Henry! I know how you feel, but...

HENRY
*(FORGETTING THEIR DELICATE, BLACK-WHITE
1849 RELATIONSHIP)*
You...know how I feel?

YANCEY
(STRONGLY)
You're damn right I do. I'm a man, same as you. I know
how I'd feel if I were in your shoes.

HENRY
(FEELING HIM OUT)
Are you sayin' you know how it feels to be a slave?

YANCEY
(WITH CONVICTION)
I would never be a slave.

SOUND
(FOOTSTEPS CLOMPING INTO THE STORE, UNDER)

CUSTOMER
(GOOD OL' BOY SPEECH PATTERN)
Hi ya doin', Bob? Looks like another warm one, huh?

YANCEY
I reckon. What can I do for ya, Seth?

CUSTOMER
Oh, justa couple plugs o' tobacky. Looks like a good day
to go hang a line out over the river.

YANCEY
Yep, great day for it, catfish oughta be feelin' downright
greedy.

206

CUSTOMER

Well, what're you waitin' for? Grab your gear'n let's . . .

YANCEY

Nope, not today, Seth, I got inventory to do. I give you permission to catch my share.

CUSTOMER

I'm sure gonna try, see ya later.

YANCEY

Take it easy, Seth.

SOUND
(CLANG/SMASH/RING OF CASH REGISTER, IN AND OUT. FOOTSTEPS CLOMPING OUT)

HENRY
(CONSPIRATORIALLY)
Mister Yancy, you just said . . . you said . . . you'd never be a slave?

YANCEY

That's right, and as you can see, I don't own any.

HENRY

You know, Mister Yancey, I been thinkin' for a long time . . . about not being a slave.

YANCEY

Oh?

HENRY

Yessir, I been thinkin' 'bout not being a slave for a good long while.

YANCEY
(COLDLY)
Does your master know anything about what you're thinkin'?

HENRY
(RUSHING INTO IT)
No, sir, you're the only one who knows and the only reason I'm tellin' you is because...

YANCEY
Careful, Henry, I think you're gittin' a lil' bit off the mark here.

HENRY
(BOLDLY)
I don't think so, Mr. Yancey...not if all the talks we've had have any truth in them. I've heard you say, from time to time, that every man is entitled to his liberty. Did you really mean that?

YANCEY
I'm a man of my word, you know that.

HENRY
Mr. Yancey, what would you say if I asked for your help to get out of Virginia, out of slavery?

YANCEY
(STIFFLY)
I'm a businessman, Henry, not a lawbreaker.

HENRY
What if we just thought of it as a business deal?

YANCEY
Well, I...uhh...

HENRY
(DRIVING ON)
I've heard you say that business is just a matter of dollars 'n cents. I've got a hundred and sixty six dollars. I'm willin' to give you all of it if you help me.

YANCEY
(HESITANTLY)
I...I don't quite know what to say, Henry...helpin' slaves run away is a serious matter.

HENRY
(EARNESTLY)
Please help me, Mister Yancey, please...I don't know anyone else I can turn to. I'm sick n tired of belongin' to somebody, like a dog or a horse. I want to be a free man.

(PAUSE)

YANCEY
Well, what can I say? I guess I'd be a hypocrite if I didn't help you, but let's not misunderstand each other, this is strictly a business deal. You say you have a hundred and sixty six dollars?

HENRY
(EXCITED)
Yessir, a hundred and sixty six dollars!

YANCEY
(COLDLY)
I'll charge you half of that, fair enough?

HENRY

More than fair, more than fair.

YANCEY

Good. Now then, let's hear your plan. What have you got in mind?

HENRY

I hadn't thought of anything, Mister Yancey, other than being free, that's the only thing that's been on my mind.

YANCEY

I understand that, Henry, but we need more than thoughts, you need a plan. In order for you to get out of Virginia, we're goin' to have to figure out a way to get you past the patrols. As you know, with that Harriet Tubman woman runnin' wild, stealin' slaves and runnin' back north with them, the patrols are pretty heavy.

HENRY

I know, I got a whippin' last week cause they caught me on the road after dark; if it hadn't been for master's note it might've been worse.

YANCEY

Well, you know how it is, lots of folks still have Nat Turner on the brain. Let's see now, what can we come up with? We've had a mulatto woman dress up like a white man and use her dark skinned husband to drive out of Georgia. Did you hear about that?

HENRY

Yessir.

YANCEY
(HUMOROUSLY)
You know any mulatto ladies with coaches that need drivers?

HENRY
(SERIOUS REACTION)
Not off hand, Mister Yancey.

YANCEY
Hmmm...today is the 15th, let's put our minds on this for a couple days and see what we can come up with.

HENRY
(FERVENTLY)
Sure do want to thank you, Mister Yancey.

YANCEY
No thanks needed, Henry. Like I said, it's strictly a business deal. You said you had the money with you?

HENRY
Oh, yes, I've got it here in my coat linin'.

YANCEY
Don't pull it out here! It wouldn't do for anyone walkin' in here to see you givin' me money. Go in the back room and place it between those two flour sacks over in the far corner.

SOUND
(THE TOBACCO FACTORY, BARRELS BEING ROLLED INTO PLACE, STACKED UNDER)

MISTER ALLEN, THE OVERSEER
Awright, Brown, look sharp there!

SOUND
(OUT)

211

MUSIC
(SLOW, RANDOM NOTES FROM A BANJO BEING TUNED, UNDER)

HOST

For the next few days Henry Brown went to work every day with a bushel full of conflicts thrashing around in his mind. Had Bob Yancey, the store keeper, simply taken his money? Could he trust him? Would he help him and then betray him? Even with help he knew that the odds against him escaping were great. The consequences for attempting to escape, he knew, were terrible. He could have an R (for runaway) branded on his face. He could have a foot chopped off. He could be given fifty lashes or a hundred, with a bull hide whip. He could be sold into the deep South, making another escape almost impossible.

He could be killed, legally, for attempting to escape.

He and Bob Yancey discussed a number of ways to escape, but a flaw was detected in each plan. Most of their plans, as carefully thought out as possible, would not have gotten him past Richmond's city limits.

The days shuffled past. Henry worked his normal twelve hour day, half asleep, his body and spirit drooping from overwork and mental stress, the thought of escaping from slavery in a box flickered in and out of his mind. And then held steady.

HENRY

A box...that's it! I could escape in a box.

MUSIC
(OUT)

YANCEY

A box?! Are you crazy?!

HENRY

No sir, slaves ain't allowed to be crazy, as you well know.

YANCEY

I get your point, Henry, I get your point. It just might not be such a bad idea, not such a bad idea at all. But a box...?

HENRY
(BITTERLY)

If I'm not free I may as well be in a box anyway.

YANCEY
(ENTHUSIASTICALLY)

I think it just might work! Tell you what, I just happen to know a man named McKim, in Philadelphia, who just happens to be a red hot Abolitionist...he'd be glad to help.

HENRY

When do I leave?

YANCEY

Hold your horses! I'll have to contact him first, to make sure he'll be available to receive you 'n all.

You wouldn't want to be stuck in the baggage room of some train station for a week, would you?

HOST

The plan agreed upon, the destination decided on, Henry set about the business of having a box built.

SOUND
(CARPENTER'S SHOP, SAWING, HAMMERING
GOING ON, UNDER)

HENRY

Mose, your master here?

MOSE
(LACONIC TONES)

Nawww, he's upstairs sleepin', fulla rum as usual. *(OFF)* Hey! Watch what you're doin'! That wood is 'sposed to be sanded with the grain, not against it! *(TO HENRY)* I don't know what to say about some o' these youngbloods, they just don't take no pride at all in their work.

HENRY
(SARCASTICALLY)

I wonder why?

MOSE

Huh?

HENRY

Oh, nothin', just talkin' to myself. Listen, Mose, I need a favor.

MOSE

How can I do you a favor? I ain't got nuthin'.

HENRY

You can do me this favor.

MOSE

Well, quit beatin' round the bush, I got work to do, spit it out.

HENRY

I want you to make a box, Mose.

MOSE
(AMUSED)

A box? You plannin' to call it a day? What kinda box.

HENRY

I want the best wood you can use, square shaped, two feet eight inches deep, two feet wide and three feet long. Make it so that the cover can be nailed on.

MOSE
(UNDERSTANDING)

Sounds like...hold on a minute, *(OFF)* Tumbee! You puttin' the door of that cabinet on upside down! Be sharp about yourself, boy!

HENRY
(APPRECIATIVELY)

You take a lotta pride in your work, don't you?

MOSE

If I didn't you wouldn't've come to me for your box. What was that size again?

HENRY

Two feet eight inches deep, two feet wide and three feet long.

MOSE

It'll be a tight squeeze, Henry.

HENRY

I know, but it's got to look like just an ordinary dry goods box. If it was any bigger it might look suspicious.

MOSE

You're right. When do you want it?

HENRY

Within two days time.

MOSE

That'd be the 28th.

HENRY

Right.

MOSE

It'll be ready on the 27th. I'll make it myself.

HENRY

I...I got a lil' money, Mose...I could...

MOSE

Keep it, Henry, you'll need it more than I will.

SOUND
(HEAVY FOOTSTEPS CLOMPING DOWNSTAIRS, UNDER)

HENRY

Thanks a heap, Mose.

MOSE
(URGENTLY)

You gonna pick this up?

HENRY

I may not be able to, is there some way you can get it over to Bob Yancey's store?

MOSE

Bob Yancey? No problem, he gets crates 'n stuff from here all the time. You better get outta here, sounds like Master Clarke is in a foul mood.

HENRY
(QUICKLY)

Thanks again, Mose. God bless you!

SOUND
(OUT)

MASTER CLARKE
(CRUDE, VICIOUS VOICE)
Awright! What's goin' on down here! Mose!?

MOSE
Yessir, Master Clarke?

MASTER CLARKE
Did I see a strange darky down here?

MOSE
No, sir, Master Clarke, we the only ones down here. *(OFF)* Hey, you there, Tumbee! Hurry on with that table top! Master Clarke promised he'd have it ready by ten o'clock tomorrow mornin'.

MASTER CLARKE
(DRUNK)
Yeahh! Git a move on 'fore I lose my temper and take my belt to you rascals!

MOSE
(SLYLY)
Ain't no need for that, Master Clarke...everything gonna be taken care of.

HOST
Henry Brown left Clarke's carpenter shop feeling more troubled than at any time since his plan had formed. This was the crucial point, the making of his box, his transportation to freedom. If Mose decided to turn him in, for whatever a slave would be rewarded for that act, all would be lost.

If any suspicions were aroused by casual observers of his actions and reported to his master or any other authority, if he suffered an attack of nerves and behaved in any way

217

that indicated that something unusual was happening in his mind, if...

All of this and more occurred to him, but he mentally shovelled it off to one side. His dream was the free life, a dim awareness of what it would mean to have the opportunity to freely use his brain, his abilities, and strength to succeed or fail without any fear of the whip or the auction block. In pursuit of a human existence he was willing to take any chance.

MUSIC
(TAMBOURINE SOLO 6/8 TIME, CURTAIN, ACT ONE)

(COMMERCIALS)

ACT TWO

HOST
If the tensions of the days and nights that Henry Brown only thought of freedom had been a strain, one can imagine how he felt on March 27, 1849, two days before his scheduled "move to the north."

YANCEY
But you don't understand, Henry. I haven't heard from my friend in Philadelphia. What happens if you get in the box, they deliver it and no one comes to collect it? You could be shipped back or starve to death, or somethin'!

HENRY
I'll die a free man, Mister Yancey.

YANCEY

(EXASPERATED)

Maybe I'm not makin' myself plain, Henry. My friend hasn't answered my letter. Now, that may mean he didn't get my letter. Or that it was lost, or...I don't know what. It's too much of a chance to take.

HENRY

I'm willin' to take that chance, Mister Yancy.

YANCEY

(PAUSE)

I can see that you are, Henry, I can see that you are. Alright, everything is set. The box is here and you're ready to go but how're you goin' to provide a cover for yourself to git away? You'll need a few hours, at least.

HENRY

(DETERMINED VOICE)

I'll manage that between today and tomorrow.

SOUND

(THE TOBACCO FACTORY, BARRELS BEING ROLLED, UNDER)

MR. ALLEN

What're you talkin' about, Brown! You done hurt your hand? You still got another one you can use! Git on back to your bench!

HOST

Henry Brown stared at his right hand, the hand he had deliberately scraped to the bone, and cussed under his breath. What would it take to get the rest of the day off, in order to have a day's start on the patrols?

(PAUSE)

HENRY

Mister Allen! Mister Allen! I done hurt my left hand too, sir!

MR. ALLEN

What?! Your left too! Lemme see!

HENRY

What can I do about it, sir?

MR. ALLEN

Well, ain't nothin' can be done for you here, looks like you've managed to knock your master out of half a day's pay. I'm sure he won't be too happy with you 'bout that. If I thought you was deliberately tryin' to sluff off on me, I'd take my whip to your backside.

HENRY
(QUICKLY)

My hands is really hurt, Mr. Allen, you can see for yourself.

MR. ALLEN
(RELUCTANTLY CONCEDING)

Yeah, guess you're tellin' the truth. Go on home and get some poultices of flax-meal and use that on 'em.

HENRY
(CONNING)

Thank you, Mister Allen.

SOUND
(OUT)

HOST

Henry walked quickly through the streets of Richmond, heading for Bob Yancey's store, his injured hands forgotten, his mind totally focused on the adventure ahead of him.

BULLY #1

Hey, boy! Come back here!

HENRY

Who, me?

BULLY #2

Yes, you! Who do you think you are?! Do you know you just walked right between us?

HENRY

Sorry, I...uh...

BULLY #1

Boy, you got a name?

HENRY
(PROTECTING HIS GETAWAY)

Yessir, Tom Washington, sir.

BULLY #2

What's your master's name?

HENRY

My master's name...?

BULLY #1

You got a master, ain't you? Or are you a runaway?

HENRY

Oh, no sir, I ain't run away, my master's name is Mister Edward Jefferson.

BULLY #2

Does your master know that you run up 'n down the streets tryin' to knock people down?

HENRY

No, sir.

BULLY #2

Oh, so you *do* try to knock people down?

HENRY
(DESPERATELY)

No, sir, I never...I mean...

BULLY #2
(ABRUPTLY)

What's that sign say? The one across the street in that window.

HENRY

Uhh, I don't know, sir...I can't read.

BULLY #1

You sure?

HENRY

Yessir.

BULLY #1

BULLY #1

Gene, you think this lil' rascal is tellin' the truth?

BULLY #2

Hard to say, ain't no tellin' 'bout the ones who run up 'n down the street tryin' to bump into people 'n whatnot. Maybe we oughta have him arrested and have his master come git him, that'd teach him a lesson.

HENRY

I'm truly sorry, it's just that Master Jefferson told me to hurry back with his snuff and I was thinkin' 'bout how...

BULLY #1

What happened to your hands?

HENRY

Master got mad and stomped on 'em cause I was too slow bringin' his hat.

BULLY #2
(LAUGHING)

Well, looks like you're in for a lil' more stompin'.

HENRY
(DULLY)

Yessir.

BULLY #1

In the future, you be sure 'n show some respect for people, you understand?

HENRY

Yessir.

BULLY #2

Now git!

SOUND
(HENRY'S HURRIED STEPS, FADE OUT)

YANCEY
(WORRIED)
Henry, I was beginnin' to think you weren't goin' to make it.

HENRY
Me too.

YANCEY
You're in luck, I just got a letter in the afternoon post from my friend in Philadelphia. He wishes us luck and promised he'd be at the depot to claim you. You'll be going by Adams Express all the way to Philadelphia. The trip should take between twenty seven and thirty seven hours, provided the handlers give your box express service all the way.

HENRY
What time do I leave?

YANCEY
4 a.m., you've got about eight hours yet. Hey, what happened to your hands?

HENRY
I had to do somethin' to get off work.

YANCEY
Come on in back, we'll put some flax meal poultices on 'em.

SOUND
(GRANDFATHER CLOCK STRIKES TEN TIMES, UNDER)

MASTER CARSON
(EDUCATED VIRGINIAN SPEECH PATTERN)
Emily, have you read the Enquirer today?

MRS. CARSON
(MAGNOLIA-BLOSSOM EDITH BUNKER TONES)
No, I haven't, dear. I've been as busy as a bee all day,
making sure the spring cleaning was being done properly.
Is there something interesting?

SOUND
(OUT)

MASTER CARSON
Couple things. There's an editorial here suggesting that the
legislature pass something called a Fugitive Slave Act. Hmf!
We wouldn't need any more laws if they put some teeth in
the ones we have.

MRS. CARSON
You're absolutely right, dear.

MASTER CARSON
And this Tubman woman! It's just down right disgraceful
that they can't catch her. Can you imagine?!...an illiterate,
runaway slave going back and forth, from north to south and
back, with a posted reward of $30,000 on her head, stealing
slaves! And they can't catch her. Disgraceful!

MRS. CARSON
It certainly is.

SOUND
(ANGRY RUSTLE OF A NEWSPAPER, IN AND OUT)

MASTER CARSON
(GRUMBLING)
What're you sewing?

MRS. CARSON

It isn't really sewing, dear, it's embroidery. I'm doing a pastoral design.

MASTER CARSON
(BACK TO THE NEWS)

Hmf!...and these Abolitionists! A bunch of hypocrites! They point their finger at us for having slaves and yet their factory system does more human harm than our system ever did. At least our people are fed and clothed, taken care of from birth to death!

MRS. CARSON

I agree, dear. They just want to abolish slavery in order to get more cheap labor for their sweat shops.

(PAUSE)

SOUND
(RUSTLE OF PAPER, IN AND OUT)

MASTER CARSON
(GRUMBLING)

Underground Railroads! Runaways! Tobacco prices down! White trash trying to buy their way into polite society. I don't know what the world is coming to. Tilly!

SOUND
(FEMININE FOOTSTEPS FADE IN)

TILLY
(BELLIGERENT BLACK VOICE)

You called, Master Carson?

MASTER CARSON

Uhh, yes, pour me a glass of Madeira.

226

TILLY

Yes, Master Carson.

SOUND
(TINKLE OF DECANTER AGAINST GLASS, GURGLE OF LIQUOR, OUT)

TILLY

Will that be all, Master Carson?

MASTER CARSON

Yes, for now.

SOUND
(FOOTSTEPS FADE OUT)

MRS. CARSON

Tilley is in a family way again, Paul.

MASTER CARSON
(SIPPING HIS DRINK)

Oh, how do you know?

MRS. CARSON
(COLD ANGER)

I think it's perfectly obvious for anyone with eyes to see.

MASTER CARSON

Well, looks like Henry...

MRS. CARSON

I don't think Henry has anything to do with it. But we shall have to wait and see, won't we? If this one is as light skinned as the last one, we'll know for certain that he had nothing to do with it.

227

MASTER CARSON
(COLDLY)

Why don't we cross that bridge when we come to it?
Mentioning Henry, has he come in yet?

MRS. CARSON

No, not yet. Mr. Allen came by to find out how his hands
were, it seems that he got hurt today.

MASTER CARSON

Hmf! Guess that's going to mean a day's loss of pay. He's
been sulking ever since his wife was sold, looks like he's
overdue for a bit of disciplining. Uh, would you care for
a glass of Madeira, my dear?

MRS. CARSON

Yes, I'll pour my own, thank you.

SOUND
(TINKLE OF DECANTER AGAINST GLASS, OUT)

YANCEY
(WHISPERING)

Henry, wake up, it's time.

HENRY

I'm not asleep, Mr. Yancey.

YANCEY

Keep your voice down, I got a man with a wagon outside
who thinks he's takin' a box of goods to the express office.
You got everything you need? You bore air holes?

HENRY

Three really small ones in each side. I think it might be a
good idea to keep the gimlet with me, just in case.

YANCEY

Good idea. Water?

HENRY

A full bladder and a few biscuits.

YANCEY

You want to take some more food?

HENRY

I won't need it, I'll save my appetite for freedom.

YANCEY

Good luck. Who knows? I might go into the box shippin'
business if you prove to be profitable.

SOUND

(APPROACHING FOOTSTEPS ON WOODEN FLOOR, UNDER)

DRAYMAN
(RAGGED VOICE)

'Bout ready to tote that outta here, Mr. Yancey?

YANCEY
(CALLING)

Just soon as I nail the cover on.

HENRY

Bless you...

SOUND

(LID BEING PLACED, RAPID HAMMERING, IN AND OUT)

YANCEY

O.K., Johnny, all set to go. You wanna come back here and
give me a hand with this?

SOUNDS

*(THEY GRUNT AND LIFT/FOOTSTEPS IN TANDEM
ON WOODEN FLOOR, UNDER)*

DRAYMAN

Pretty fair sized load, huh, Mr. Yancey?

YANCEY

Yep, that's the way it is, Johnny. Them Yankee ladies hate
our guts but they love our cotton cloth.

SOUND

*(BOX BEING PLACED ON A WAGON,
HORSE SNORTS, OUT)*

DRAYMAN

There we go . . .

YANCEY

Remember, Johnny, try to keep the side up that's marked.
I'd kinda like to keep the stuff inside straight.

DRAYMAN

Do my best, Mr. Yancey, do my best. Giddup!

SOUND

*(HORSE SLOWLY CLOPPING AWAY,
WAGON WHEELS CREAKING, UNDER)*

YANCEY
(SOFTLY)

Good luck to you, Henry Brown.

SOUND

(HORSES/CREAKY WHEELS CONTINUE, UNDER)

HENRY
(INTROSPECTIVELY)

After a few minutes I felt like screamin,' Let me out! Let me out. I can't stand being cooped up in here!...cramped into a sittin' position with just enough room for me to move my arms a bit, and shift my weight slightly, whenever one position became tiresome. From Bob Yancey's store to the Express Office was a mile. It's a mile I'll never forget.

Goin' that mile, stuffed up in that lil' wooden box, I had a chance to go back through everything that had ever happened to me.

Most of what came to mind was pretty ugly; not knowin' who my momma 'n daddy was because we had been sold off to different folks. I thought about being whipped out to work before the sun came up, havin' barely enough to eat and hardly enough clothes to cover my body, even in the wintertime.

Work, all the time, work. A field hand. I had been a field hand under an overseer who was so mean that he used to whip peoples' eyes out of their heads. Master liked that cause he could get so much work out of the hands. Didn't matter how we was treated, he could work or beat us to death and buy a new batch.

They said that none of the field hands had ever lived longer than five years on this man's plantation. I was in my third year when he died. Some say Dicey, the cook, put shaved glass in his food. Master Carson bought me into the city and hired me out. He probably saved my life. I don't think I could've lasted too much longer. Yeahhh, he probably saved my life but I couldn't be too grateful because I was still a slave.

A whole bunch o' things went through my mind travelin' that mile to the Express Office.

I prayed. I prayed to Almighty God for salvation, that He

231

should not let me get caught and taken back. I was so scared
I didn't know what to do. I tried to see what freedom would
look like in my mind, but it was too dark.

DRAYMAN
(REINING IN)

Whoa!

SOUND
(HORSE/WAGON CREAK TO A STOP, OUT)

DRAYMAN

You there! You! With the fuzzy eyeballs! C'mon over here
'n he me with this crate.

SOUND
*(STEPS RUSHING OVER/BOX BEING
LIFTED OFF OF WAGON, OUT)*

STATION CLERK

What we got here, Phillydelphia, huh?

DRAYMAN

That's what it says, clear as day.

SOUND
*(STATION CLERK STAMPS "DESTINATION
PHIL, PA" ON THE BOX, OUT)*

HENRY

From havin' seen it done on shipments of tobacco casks, I
knew that the station clerk had stamped where I was goin'
on my box. My heart was so far up in my throat I could
hardly swallow.

Somebody came along after a lil' while, lifted my box and
tipped me over into a baggage car, upside down.

After a few minutes of being on my head, I felt my eyes

about to pop out and the blood fillin' up the veins in my temple made my head feel like it was about to explode. My whole body went into a cold sweat and I just knew I was goin' to die. I just knew it. That was the feelin' I had.

As the train started steamin' up to go, I prayed with all my might that I would be saved from the torture of stayin' on my head.

SOUND
(TRAIN CHUG CHUGGING/STEAMING UP FOR DEPARTURE)

MUSIC
(CURTAIN, ACT II)

(COMMERCIALS)

ACT THREE

SOUND
(CLACKETY CLACK OF TRAIN ENROUTE, UNDER)

HENRY
The Lord answered my prayers. Somebody, pushin' 'n movin' stuff around, just 'fore the train started, in order to make more room for some other baggage, laid me over on my side. It look a lil' while for my blood to right itself, for the veins in my head to go down . . . but after while I felt like myself again.

I was alright for a while, just bumpin' along with all the rest of the crates and baggage, til this dull ache started up and down my right side, the side I was layin' on.

I could shift my weight off of my shoulder joint by a little, to get some of the pressure off, but mostly I had a heavy,

233

dull feelin'.

I just completely lost track o' time. I tried goin' backwards to when I had started out, at 4 a.m., to try to guess what time it might be. I just couldn't figure past a certain point. It didn't matter no way, time was standin' still for me. The heat of the box was really bad and my clothes was soakin' wet from sweat. From time to time, I would close my eyes and try to think of somethin' else, a good time I had, or somethin' like that.

I couldn't do it. I'd come close a few times but then, a hard, tight feelin' would grab the muscles in my stomach and knock everything else out.

I did think strong on my wife, Maylene. I cried a lil' bit, thinkin' about her being lost from me, with no way for me to ever see her again.

I felt bad, deep down, about runnin' away by myself.

I had talked to her about runnin' away but she was always afraid of what would happen if we got caught.

At one point I thought I was dead. It just didn't seem that I could possibly be alive, hardly able to move, sweat drippin' off me like rainwater, every muscle stiff from being locked in place.

I clenched my teeth together and tightened my messed up hands into fists and prayed.

I prayed to God to give me the strength to hold out, to keep my mind together and not crack.

It was like being in a hole somewhere. The box became a part of my skin and I wanted to pull my skin off but I couldn't because my skin was the box.

I became confused. My mind wouldn't work right. Had I been in the box a day, or two days? Was I goin' in the right direction? What would happen to me if my box was going South instead of North? If somebody had made a mistake.

Somehow I could see myself in a baggage room somewhere, slowly starvin' to death, because I made a vow on my soul's damnation that I would rather be dead than be a slave again. I have never felt more lonely in my life than I felt at that moment.

SOUND
(TRAIN, FADES OUT)

SOUND
(GRANDFATHER CLOCK STRIKES NINE TIMES, UNDER)

MR. ALLEN
(SERVILE TONES)
Mighty sorry to disturb you folks at breakfast, Mister Carson, Miz Carson...

SOUND
(OUT)

MASTER CARSON
I was coming to see you, Allen, right after breakfast.

MRS. CARSON
Would you care for a cup of coffee, Mr. Allen?

MR. ALLEN
Uhh, no thanks, m'am, I et a while ago.

MASTER CARSON
(IMPATIENTLY)
Well, let's get to the point, Allen, it's about Henry, isn't it?

MR. ALLEN
Yessir. I suspected somethin' tricky was goin' on when I come by yestiddy evenin' to check 'n see if he was givin' his hands the proper treatment.

MASTER CARSON
(RAGE BUILDING)

So, he hasn't been here and he hasn't been to work. You think he's a runaway?!

MR. ALLEN

'Pears to be, sir, from the looks o' things.

MASTER CARSON
(EXPLODING)

The nerve of that little...!

SOUND
*(COFFEE CUPS RATTLE AS HE POUNDS
ON THE TABLE OUT)*

MRS. CARSON

Now, now, Paul...you mustn't excite yourself.

MASTER CARSON
(IGNORES HER, FURIOUS)

I'm going to have him caught! I'm going to have him caught and whipped to within an inch of his life!

MR. ALLEN

I'd kinda like to see him after you finish with him, it ain't ever day that I git the wool pulled over my eyes.

MASTER CARSON

The nerve of him! After I bought him off the Braxton plantation, saved him would be a better way to put it! Gave him a chance to hire out!

MR. ALLEN

Well, just goes to show ya how ungrateful these...

236

MRS. CARSON
(DELICATELY)

Please, Mister Allen...

MR. ALLEN

Oops, sorry, m'am. Well, I gotta run along, lots o' work to do.

MASTER CARSON

Wait, I'll walk out with you. I'm going to have a wanted ad placed in the Enquirer.

SOUND
(MEN'S FOOTSTEPS FADE, OUT/DOOR CLOSED, OUT)

SOUND
(TRAIN FADES IN, GRINDS TO A STOP, HISS OF STEAM, OUT)

HENRY

From the way I was bumped I knew we had come to a stop. The freight train doors was slid open and I could hear voices and the sound of water.

SOUND
(CONFUSED MUDDLE OF VOICES, SLAPPING OF WATER, UNDER

HENRY

I was sure that I had reached the Potomac, which meant that I was headed in the right direction, at least. My spirits picked up. I really felt I had a chance to make it.

The next thing I knew I had been carried onto a boat and turned up on my head again. I just broke down and cried, I couldn't help myself.

SOUND
(STEAMBOAT PADDLES THRASHING
THROUGH WATER, UNDER)

HENRY

The motion of the boat, bouncin' back and forth, rubbed the top of my head and gave me a fiercesome headache. I don't know how long I was in that position, it could've been an hour or four. I don't know.

The bouncin' caused me to be sick and I came close to drownin' in my own bile. But I prayed for the strength to carry on, to be saved and, once again, my prayers were answered. A couple sailors, lookin' for a place to loaf, came into the place where I was.

SOUND
(FOOTSTEPS, IN AND OUT)

SAILOR #1

This one'll do, just the right size. You got the cards?

SAILOR #2

I got the cards, you bring all the money you need to lose?

SAILOR #1

Hah! That's what I like, a born loser who never gives up.

SAILOR #2

Nothin's cheaper than talk, I'll let my kings 'n queens speak for me. Here, help me lay this on its side.

SOUND
(SLAM OF THE BOX ONTO ITS SIDE, OUT)

HENRY

It took all of my will power to keep myself from screamin'
when they slammed me onto my side, but...at least I was
off my head. I thanked the good Lord and the two sailors
for that.

Somehow it seemed that I could feel the weight of their
bodies on the box. I could hardly breathe from the excitement
of knowin' that the slightest noise would give me away.

They played a lively game of cards, slammin' their cards
onto the box, drummin' their heels against the sides 'n all.

SAILOR #1

There, take that! *(CARD SLAPPING BOX SURFACE)* So, talk
is cheap, huh?!

SAILOR #2

That's right, bub! I think my ace, king and jack o' hearts
beats the stuffin' outta your ten o' clubs, jack o' spades and
queen o' diamonds!

SAILOR #1
(DISGUSTED)

Awwww! Just pure luck!

SAILOR #2

If that's all it takes to beat you, I'm satisfied.

HENRY

Durin' the course of their play on my box, a fly got inside
through one of the air holes I had bored in the sides. That
fly caused me a heap o' pure misery. It must've been one
o' those stingin' river flies cause everywhere it crawled it
bit. It lit on my nose and walked up the middle of my nose
to my forehead and back to the tip of my nose again, stingin'
all the way. It crawled across my left eyelid and my right

eyelid, my lips, in and out of my right ear. I was tortured by the fly somethin' awful and there was nothin' I could do about it. I was afraid to try to squash it for fear that I'd make a noise and be discovered. Finally...

SAILOR #1
We better get back on deck, first mate'll be hoppin' mad if he can't find us, besides, I think you got 'bout as much of my money as I wanna lose today.

SAILOR #2
Like I said, talk is cheap, better luck next time.

SOUND
(STEAMBOAT WHISTLE, OUT)

HENRY
Strange thing happened. The minute those sailors left, the fly left too. I don't know where it went but I was very happy that it went wherever it went. I had the sailors to thank for takin' me off my head and placin' me on my side. But, as you can well imagine, being in that position grew pretty tiresome too, after awhile. Hope, prayer and the belief that my journey would have to come to an end, for better or worse, kept me alive.

And then, as though some miracle had happened, I heard somebody say, "Yep, that's Washington."

(PAUSE)

SOUND
*(SHUFFLING ON WOODEN FLOOR OF
BOB YANCEY'S STORE, OUT)*

MR. ALLEN

That's right, completely disappeared! Ol' man Carson's fit to be tied!

YANCEY

What about the hounds?

MR. ALLEN

Ain't got no scent to work from. They took a sniff off some of his ol' clothes 'n ever one of 'em started off in a diff'rent die-rection. Lemme me have a slug on that jug, Clarke.

CUSTOMER

Now this is 'bout the dawgonest thing I ever heard of, ain't a human body made what could disappear into thin air.

YANCEY
(ENJOYING HIMSELF)

Everybody's thinkin' he went North, maybe he went South.

MASTER CLARKE
(DRUNKEN SLUR)

Awww c'mon, Bob, ain't a darky in this state that would run South.

MR. ALLEN

Sayyy, you know somethin', Bob, you might have a point. He might head South, to throw everybody off the track and then head North.

CUSTOMER

If he did it'd be the first time I ever heard o' such.

YANCEY

I'll take a swig o' that. Who knows? Ain't no tellin' what a man'll do when he decides to run away.

HENRY

I was unloaded and placed on a wagon, right side up. I was crazy to take a look at all the hustle 'n bustle I could hear, to take a look at things, maybe see what Washington looked like, but I had drilled the holes up high on the box in order to keep people from peekin' in.

Bumpin' along in the wagon to the train depot, I passed a section where I could smell greens, side meat, candied yams, hush puppies and barbeque. The smells made my mouth water.

I realized I was hungrier than I had been in quit a while. I managed to fumble a couple soggy biscuits in my mouth and drink a little water. Washington seemed to be hotter than any place I'd been in my box so far.

HENRY

We were at the train depot, I could hear train sounds like in Richmond and somebody jumpin' up on the wagon to unload it. The way I figured it, I had two more times to be unloaded, this time and when we got to Philadelphia. I felt like a wet dishrag.

FREIGHTMAN #1

Hey, Boomer! Gimme a hand with this box!

FREIGHTMAN #2

I'm busy, push it off and drag it on over to the loadin' platform.

FREIGHTMAN #1

But it's got this...uhh..."this side up with care" marked on it.

FREIGHTMAN #2

Awww, who cares?! The company can make it good if you break anything.

SOUND

(BOX CRASHING TO THE GROUND, OUT)

HENRY

The next thing I knew I had this feelin' of fallin' through the air. My neck made a cracky sound when the box hit the ground and I was knocked out of my mind for a while.

I was about ready to give up, I didn't feel I could take anymore, 'specially after I heard the two freight hands discussin' whether or not they had enough room for my box. Another man, a bossman, checking on things, came by and told them to put my box on the train.

STATION CLERK

(AUTHORITATIVELY)

This box is labeled express and it's goin' express, now move it!

SOUND

(CLAKETY CLACK OF TRAIN MOVING, UNDER)

HENRY

I was loaded on the train and on my way within a short while, my neck, my whole body bruised and achin', I was halfway out of my senses most of the time. I felt like beatin' my fists against the walls of the box to ask somebody to get me out but I was too weak. And besides, no body would've heard me in the baggage car anyway.

It seemed to me, when the train slowed and I knew we were in Philadelphia, it seemed that I had been in this box all of my natural life.

SOUND
(TRAIN CRUNCHES TO A STOP, OUT)

HENRY

Philadelphia! I made it! But I still had to be careful. I could be discovered still, and taken right straight back to Virginia. They had had cases of that happenin' to runaways. Slave catchers was always hangin' round train depots.

I was unloaded and placed with the other freight. I could feel other boxes being bumped against me.

SOUND
(THUMP/BUMP OF CRATES, IN AND OUT)

HENRY

Would the man who was supposed to claim the box come? Did we have some kind of mix up about times or dates?

A thousand doubts played on my mind. Maybe I would simply remain wherever I was until I died. My neck felt like it was broken and I was seein' red spots in front of my eyes.

I had come a long way and yet I was nowhere.

It seems that I was there, thinkin' all these kinds of thoughts, for an awful long time before I felt my box being moved. Someone had come to claim me. Man had an Irish

244

voice.

DAN
(DELIVERYMAN, IRISH BROGUE)
I'm here to pick up a box from Richmond, Virginia, for Dr. McKim. Here's the receipt.

HENRY
I was once again loaded on a wagon, head up this time, thank God! and hauled away. By now I felt I could hang on a lil' longer.

The Irish voice delivered me to a house.

DAN
That's a heavy box, Dr. McKim.

DR. McKIM
Thank you, Dan. *(TIPS HIM)*

DAN
Thank you, sir.

HENRY
I could hear people around the box and then a knockin'.

SOUND
(KNOCK! KNOCK! OUT)

DR. McKIM
Are you alive, inside there?

HENRY
(CRACKED, SHAKY VOICE)
Yes, yes, I'm alive.

SOUND
(FRANTIC PULLING OF NAILS, COVER BEING TAKEN OFF)

SOUNDS
(GASPS, EXCLAIMATIONS FROM THE FOUR MEN AROUND THE BOX, OUT)

DR. McKIM
Oh my God! Catch him before he falls!

HENRY
(SHAKY, BUT TRIUMPHANT)
I'll be awright, sir...just a lil' weak, but I'll be awright now, I'm a free man.

HOST
Some of the details of the story we have just heard were altered, the dialogue invented, but the basic truth is this: on March 29, 1849, a slave named Henry Brown had himself nailed into a box in Richmond, Virginia, traveled three hundred and fifty odd miles in twenty-seven hours to Philadelphia, Pennsylvania, and was uncrated by Dr. J. M. McKim, Professor C.D. Cleveland, Mr. Lewis Thompson and Mr. William Still, Abolitionists.

They nicknamed him "Box," and that is the name by which we know him today: Mr. Henry "Box" Brown.

MUSIC
(CURTAIN)

"Mr. Henry "Box" Brown was written by *Chester L. Simmons* produced and directed by *Odie Hawkins.*